"Say someone came along that seemed to be Messiah. What if you caught him in the wings, while he was waiting to go onstage?" Thatcher's eyes held the light, shining like beacons, cleaving the dark. "How would you effect a co-opt? Could you interface him into the corporate frame? How much weight could he throw in the marketplace?"

"What if he's not—"

"Say he isn't anything but a good talker with the look," said Thatcher. "So? Doesn't mean he can't get things done with our help. If the idea's too—what's the word I want—"

"Crazy."

"Transcendent," he said. "With a little coaching, fellow like Macaffrey could do us a world of good. Show him which side to put the butter on. How to slice up the loaf."

"What if he is the messiah?" I asked. "What then?"

Thatcher walked across the room to look over his land, staring into Long Island's crimson air. "Different runway," he said. "Same approach." He turned to watch me zip my skirt. "Heathen might just get what they want for a change, or what they think they want."

Heathern, the word emerged, mangled by his accent. All were heathern in his eyes; had they become so in mine as well?

HEATHERN
by Jack Womack

"An entirely original American voice!"

— William Gibson, author of *Neuromancer*

Tor books by Jack Womack

Terraplane
Heathern

HEATHERN

JACK WOMACK

A TOM DOHERTY ASSOCIATES BOOK
NEW YORK

HEATHERN

Copyright © 1990 by Jack Womack

Cover art by Nicholas Jainschigg

A Tor Book
Published by Tom Doherty Associates, Inc.
49 West 24th Street
New York, N.Y. 10010

ISBN: 0-812-50872-6

First edition: September 1990
First mass market printing: June 1991

Printed in the United States of America

0 9 8 7 6 5 4 3 2 1

For Nancy
With Nancy knows what,
and Nancy knows why.

From a report of the 2nd Battalion, 405th Infantry, U.S. Army, April 1945:

We discovered near Gardelegen an atrocity so awful that it might well have been committed in another era, or indeed, on another planet.

ONE

· · · ·

A baby almost killed me as I walked to work one morning. By passing beneath a bus shelter's roof at the ordained moment I lived to tell my tale. With strangers surrounding me I looked at what remained. Laughter from heaven made us lift our eyes skyward. The baby's mother lowered her arms and leaned out her window. Without applause her audience drifted off, seeking crumbs in the gutters of this city of God. Xerox shingles covered the shelter's remaining glass pane, and the largest read:

Want to be crucified. Have own nails.
Leave message on machine.

The fringe of numbers along the ad's hem had been stripped away. My shoes crunched glass underfoot; my skirt

1

clung to my legs as I continued down the street. November dawn's seventy-degree bath made my hair lose its set. Mother above appeared ready to take her own bow; I too, as ever, flew on alone.

"Joanna," Thatcher said, prying loose my memory's coils that I might freely return to my present. "You want your face to freeze like that?" Thatcher Dryden, who with his wife Susie owned the Dryden Corporation—that is to say, Dryco—was my boss; my owner, in the conceptual sense. As Vice President in charge of New Projects I rarely listened during the morning rundowns, as I had yet to work on a new project in the nine months since he promoted me. "There's something I want you to look at tomorrow. See if anything's there."

"Anything where?" I asked. Thatcher's eyes glazed, as if he imagined me clad in one of those specialized designs he favored, the sort I refused to wear.

"Got some reports in about some fellow on the Lower East Side—"

"Loisaida," said Bernard. "For appearance's sake we should pretend to keep the names straight." As Vice President overseeing Operations, Bernard made sure that when his owners left teeth beneath their pillows at night they would in morning find shiny prizes in their place. He also still handled those New Projects. I'd worked under Bernard before coming to Dryco, through his mentorship learning the skills I no longer used.

"Whatever they're calling it this week," said Thatcher. "Give her the lowdown as we've got it, Bernard."

Bernard was forty-five, three years older than me; he held his printout that he might see over the frames of his bifocals, and read aloud, translating the jargon in which all paperwork, for obfuscatorial reasons, was written. "One Lester Hill Macaffrey, age twenty-nine, from Kentucky, present address unknown—"

"Squattin' somewhere, no doubt. We'll dig him up like a

clam if we have to. A Southerner, you'll notice," said Thatcher, keen to note his countryfolk.

"Turn over any rock and find one," murmured Susie Dryden, seated as ever at the far end of the table reading the *Daily News,* her eyes flitting over the pages, looking for referents, seeking in mundane reports the usable connections that underlie seemingly unrelated events; she reminded me of a hawk searching meadows for mice. Her paper's headline read: PROBLEM? THEY ASKED/CANNIBAL, HE SAID. *Kept Hand in Pocket.*

"He teaches philosophy and theology at a parent-run facility on Ninth Street," Bernard said. "Most of his students are Long Island transferees, including test group children—" Susie grimaced.

"Macaffrey teaches grade schoolers philosophy?" I asked.

"Nothing more eschatological than Nietzsche, I'm led to understand," Bernard said. "Our friends in the appropriate agencies have examined possibilities mentioned concerning potential political disruption and feel we're being quote, paranoid, unquote."

"Told you that's what they'd say," Thatcher said, placing a finger to his lips that he might hush his own classroom. "Listen now. That's all I ask."

"Said neighborhood is rife with tales of Macaffrey," Bernard continued, "most arising during the past year, most claiming that he possesses, or is possessed by, some supernatural force. It's sworn by many that through unknown agencies he provides his charges and their families with drugs—"

"Drugs? What drugs?"

Bernard winked at me. "Food, clothing, shelter. Traditional silencers. As so many these days are mad for apocalypse no matter how arbitrarily timed, more outré stories have begun to circulate, silly even by Nasty Nineties standards and far beyond most recent fin-de-sièclivities—"

3

"English, Bernard," said Thatcher.

"Sources claim he foresees and tells of the future." Bernard smiled. "Must be a fount of joy for his neighbors. Supposedly he restores sight to the blind. As predictable within such subcultures a consistent belief is that he changes the weather to suit or punish as he pleases. I don't think these tales can supply his public with the fix they need much longer. Any day now we'll probably hear stories that he's cured millions of cancer, turned water into Coca-Cola and parted the East River to ease the shipment of weapons into Brooklyn."

"Damn good research," said Thatcher. "Good talking. Thanks, Bernard."

I remembered how so often to me Bernard referred to Thatcher only as Stonewall's revenge. "It sounds so charismatic," I said. "So cultish."

"The snakecharmer's air clings to him," said Bernard. "These types rise up in ebullient times such as ours as scum rises on stew. Good to have an accomplished hand lifting the lid now and then to see what's boiling up."

"I got a hunch about this one," said Thatcher, making a series of tiny x's on his notepad with his pen.

"Like the hunch you had about that fool last May?" asked Susie.

"Messages from beyond could be useful even if true, depending on the beyond," said Bernard. "At least Swami Lester doesn't claim to have once lived in Atlantis. So many do you'd think the weight of the populace was what sunk the place."

"Makes him more believable, doesn't it?" Thatcher asked. "You got to follow these things up." Spring's oracle had professed the ability to lift the shrouds from Elvis. When he conjured up no incubus of higher rank than one claiming to have been Grover Cleveland's postmaster general, Thatcher felt more assured that Elvis was still alive, or at least for now sat waiting in the lounge of heaven's airstrip until he heard the boarding call for the return flight to earth. "This boy didn't come calling on us, it's cost-free so far. If there's something usable he's got it'll be a damn smart investment, getting in on the ground floor."

"Send a magician along," said Susie. "A *stage* magician. Someone who recognizes tricks and lies and knows what to do about them."

Bernard, stonefaced, lifted his hand. Thatcher smiled, ogling me for the tenth time that morning, his attitude implying that he'd told all of his classmates a secret I'd asked him not to tell. "Go down there tomorrow, hon. See if his shoes match his suit. Report to me once you get back."

"May we proceed?" Susie asked. "More pressing matters require notice." She turned to Gus, who'd thus far remained silent. Gus oversaw Security, and so spoke only of matters about which we didn't want to hear. He was in his sixties, and worked for many in many ways before signing on with Dryco. "Fact me on this Jensen thing, Gus."

"Mister Jensen, who worked with Latin American accounts—"

"Dog bites man," muttered Thatcher. "Who doesn't?"

"—left Chicago two nights ago, arriving at the Newark terminal on our jet number 12AR6. Jake and I were to bring him into town and we met him there." Jake was Gus's protégé and trainee. "It startled me, how pale he looked, but Jensen said he was fine. I sat with him in the back, Jake sat with the driver. Halfway through the Holland Tunnel he clutched his chest and slumped. A coronary, I thought, and pulled him closer to me. When I tried to place the oxygen mask over his mouth he pushed it away. His face was gray and blue. He felt very cold. He spoke."

"What did he say?"

"'Can you keep a secret?' he asked. I said 'Yes, my friend.' He could keep a secret as well and said nothing else. He entered a paralytic state, almost a coma. In his eyes you could tell he was thinking." Gus sighed.

"What's the moral to the tale?" Susie asked.

"None, so far," said Gus. "Our doctors examined him after he was admitted to our ward at Beekman. Within an hour he died. Poison, the doctors said."

"What poison introduced how?"

"Fugu," said Gus, "derived from a Caribbean species of blowfish—"

Thatcher nodded. "How much was Jensen allowed to know? He must have been aboveboard if he was using one of our planes."

"High enough," said Bernard. "Sometimes I saw him at various dos, forever resembling a librarian on speed. Just the same he was vouchsafed and seemed no less competent than the rest. Probably at some stage he simply took the wrong path in life."

"No ifs about it," said Thatcher. "Sushi boys are in the bush."

Bernard frowned, and when he spoke his offering was no less serious than I would have expected. "If those little yellow people weren't so little they'd be easier to spot."

"They hid on Guam for thirty years after the war," said Thatcher.

"We believe the poison was on a projectile fired into the back of the leg, behind the knee, by means of a nondiscernible microbioinoculator," Gus said. "Dartgun," he added, seeing that none of us save Bernard knew what he meant. "Easily concealed within an umbrella, for example. In a car exhaust, in a child's party whistle. Innocence doesn't deny death."

"Sounds like Russian tomfoolery to me," said Bernard, examining his nails. Whenever he dieted he fed upon his fingertips to supply the calories forbidden. "Those crazy Krasnayas eat up those Bond movies. I've often told you it's our Moscow trolls we should keep a closer eye on—"

"They need the business too bad," said Thatcher. "We're partners, boy. Russia's at war with the country, not us."

"The recovered pellet fits instruments of Cuban make," said Gus, his own Cuban accent shading his soft voice.

Thatcher shook his head. "They're in the damned Caribbean," he said. "Finally getting into the market."

"Quit fixating," said Susie.

"You've no reason to suspect," I said. "All somebody has to do is say Tokyo and you act as if samurai were running down Fifth Avenue."

"Stick to your assigned projects, hon," Thatcher told me. "You know something about conspiracy we don't?"

"Returning to this supposed conspiracy of which we have no evidence," Bernard said, "if Jensen was into freebooty he may well have been flying solo."

"Loose cannons sink ships," said Susie.

"Somebody else was involved, since somebody killed him," said Thatcher. "Wish to hell I could remember the bastard. These low-level boys, it's like looking at ants—"

"He was higher on the hill than that," said Susie. "Investigation's essentialled."

"Of course it is," said Thatcher. "You can bet Japs'll be holding the dartgun when we catch 'em. Talk about watching too many Bond movies. Fugu poison, my ass—"

"You're such an idiot, Thatcher," shouted Susie; her snow-pale skin darkened as if she'd been rinsed in cheap wine. Whenever her control over anything slackened Susie rushed to teeter wildly at hysteria's edge so that one among those who watched might rescue her as she desired. Since aligning with her husband, Susie lived by her balance. "Aren't there plots enough without your making up ones that don't exist?" Standing, she walked to the window to sightsee while biding her time; it was Bernard, and not Thatcher, who spoke anew.

"Let's forget Pearl Harbor long enough to approach this logically. Why not?"

"Give it a try," said Thatcher.

"The negotiations at Kyoto have been ongoing for a year and a half—"

"Year and eight months," said Susie, without looking at us.

"On Tuesday you'll be meeting with the closest Japan has to your equivalent—"

"Oswego—?"

"Otsuka," said Bernard. "You know his name, use it. He's the one who made the bid to us and he's worth hearing. Nothing wrong with forming with Japan the same sort of benevolently hostile relationship we have with Russia, and with Japan there'll be no need for military interaction. So long as we postnet options—"

"English," said Thatcher.

"What will Japan matter in ten, twenty years? China's learned its lesson. Once they attain production levels of even half-strength everything will be left in the dust. Then all we'll have to do for the Japanese is draw up their retirement program."

"Like they don't have enough to retire on. Property, farms, factories, stores, banks—"

"All of those assets frozen since the troubles," said Bernard. "We do the deal, then apply the blowtorch. We receive a thirty percent cut of their future profits in all aboveground American-based operations—"

"Thirty percent," Susie repeated. "He bit?"

"With all teeth. Once we sign we will have to abide by the agreement. No clowning about later on. That's our sole requirement—"

"Sounds good," said Thatcher. "Too good."

Susie stood before Gus, sounding more tranquil as she spoke. "Security's on double alert?"

"Absolutely. All guards are undergoing allegiance checks. Master Dryden is safe at your house in Westchester."

"It's Wednesday," Thatcher said. "Settle this Jensen thing by Monday, if possible. Get the police to make pertinent arrests when necessary."

"We've surrounded the usual," said Gus. "The actual assassin may prove untraceable."

"Wouldn't be the first time," said Thatcher, regarding Gus until our guard looked away.

"There's so much else that needs attention," Susie said, rubbing her forehead as if shifting her brain's patterns into bizthink; as she eased into her traditional role even her speech began to change. "What's tagged for intersits? List me." Intersits were, in our economical shorthand, international situations. Thatcher shook his head, patently displeased with the grate of neology.

"Three point seven million imperial gallons at our Vancouver plant primed for disposal," said Bernard, reading from a different printout. "Dispersal, excuse me."

"As what?" Thatcher asked. "Cancer in a jug?"

"Barter unfeasibled in *this* instance," said Bernard, resting his chin in his palm. "Call it charity."

"Third-world writeoff," said Susie. "Next."

"Dryco's Caracas unit to return online January first—"

"December fifteenth," she said.

"They ever figure out what happened?" Thatcher asked.

"Major malfunction," said Bernard. A guess; no one was left alive to ask. I gazed into Thatcher's face as if to divine the future; found myself again unsuccessful as a seeress. His actions were forever unpredictable, but this day's whim especially puzzled, that he should make advances to a teacher in a ghetto. Beyond his stated claim I could discern no higher purpose in his intentions.

"What's this I heard about some delay in the wall?" Thatcher asked. "What's up?"

"The river." Workfare recipients built the wall that would shield downtown from rising waters in the event Green-

9

house predictions proved accurate. Without working they received no government assistance; for twelve daily hours they received thirty cents. There was a two month wait for spaces that forever reopened. "Higher tides this fall than expected. At Cortlandt Street they ran out of bedrock, Schist one of those things." He paused, as if hoping for a reaction other than the one he drew forth with his pun, before reading on. "Struck quicksand at forty feet. Geologists are insisting that additional tests be performed—"

Thatcher's finger rapped my knee as if he was testing to see if I'd gone bad. He slipped a note to me beneath the table.

"Check it out, Bernard, whatever they say." *I want to see you tonight,* his note read. On the message's reverse I scribbled my reply and passed it back, peripherally watching his reaction. Thatcher glanced at it, his dark eyes fixed. His features could have been called Lincolnesque, had Lincoln been forty pounds heavier, beardless, and worn his hair tied in a short pony in the back. "Precautions. Can't trust nobody on faith."

Not tonight, he'd read.

I agreed to drink with them after work; so long as Susie accompanied he usually kept his passions reined. During this season, I settled for such company as would keep me. Through the years, spending the Thanksgiving–Hanukkah–Christmas circuit carving turkey rolls instead of turkeys, decorating bushes rather than trees, I should have convinced myself without reminder that each new year's holidays might prove more memorable than those preceding, but no; the mind rejects too many lies as the body rejects too many sleeping pills.

"What a beautiful sunset," Thatcher remarked as we rode the few blocks from Wall Street to Fraunces Tavern. Slivers of sky between buildings showed half-glimpsed glory. Old downtown's narrow streets held a medieval feel, hemmed in as they were by stone battlements and wide walls. Evening's lingering heat slapped our faces as we stepped from our car; we saw two visigoths who'd long before invaded the city, bond traders giggling as over a bug in a bottle while they poked umbrellas into a trashbag. The bag groaned; the man within hid his face with his hands.

"Amateurs," Thatcher muttered, evincing as much concern as I or anyone I knew evinced toward those who'd lost that we might win. Thatcher's snow queen, Bernard laughingly called me: ice princess, glacier girl, the hoar with heart of frost. Was I better than Thatcher for having noticed but not remarking? That was another lie I couldn't keep down. My generation's zeitgeist preferred to haunt its halls alone, without undue consideration of an unlikely heaven: therefore, like all, I saw but didn't see, cared yet didn't care; couldn't stop long enough to think about what I might do if I tried; convinced myself that there was nothing I could do, and so did nothing.

Susie took Thatcher's arm as we entered, holding him tight; he didn't pull away. He'd had involvements before ours, yet Susie never left him, nor did he want her to go. They never spoke of their unavoidable symbiosis, as if embarrassed to admit that neither could have dealt with their world by themselves. There would be no breaking of their ring from without; I'd tired of battering myself, trying. Soon enough, I believed—wanted to believe—I would fly away from it all, not knowing how, not knowing when; wanting in the meantime only to let what moments we had left together pass silently away, that he wouldn't notice I'd left till I'd gone.

Our drinks were on our booth's table. Gus sipped from each before we drank. He and Jake—who had accompanied us here—took the outer seats, walling us off from the crowd. Jake brushed debris from my corner of the booth and

I sat across from the Drydens. Susie looked at her husband as if recounting the ways she'd loved him.

"I hate this place," she said. "These animals."

"Can't isolate yourself all the time, darlin'," he said. "Look at poor old Elvis. It's the courtiers kill the king."

"Fuck Elvis," she said. "Look at you. Mister man of the people. Some man."

"Some people." Something brushed my foot; I jerked it away, having seen rats in better places. Beneath oak beams, amid tankards and pewter and steel engravings were hundreds at drudgeful play. A post-teen broker barked, crawling on his fours, his tie sweeping the floor; two women armwrestled, their flowcharts forgotten, keeping their sneakered feet firm against their chairs as each struggled to toss the other; I-bankers shook breadsticks at one another as if casting untried spells. An aging mentor at barside held forth before his adminassists and executaries, forking his hand into a cheese-ball, licking his fingers clean as he spoke. Any abomination was excusable so long as you lived in New York.

Gus illustrated a proper table setting with the unused dinnerware for Jake; to his mind social graces were as essential as social control. "Salad fork always to the left of the regular fork," he explained.

"AO," said Jake, examining the tines of both. Something returned to caress my leg. Slipping off his shoe so as not to ruin my hose, Thatcher ran his foot along my calves, appearing to his audience so expertly vacant that he might have been running for office.

"Anyone here might try and do the do," said Susie, rescuing her olives, drying her hand by rubbing her short hair, hoping perhaps to bleach the gray into platinum tones. "Pop out of the crowd and bingo. You know that." Gus frowned; in this season he wore his memories so poorly. "What are you trying to prove?"

"Not trying to prove nothing, darlin'. Just enjoying myself while I can," he said, his foot writhing over my knees. I froze, showing nothing to anyone. I dreamed of assassinating him when he prodded my thighs with his toes. "It's the edge that makes life worthwhile. Dancing through the minefields of life. Like flying over the border at night with all the lights off. Like dropping in on the competition when they're not expecting company. Just cause somebody lives straight doesn't mean they don't need a rush now and then."

"You're such a fool—"

"Too damn paranoid, darlin', that's your problem," he said, laughing. "My boys don't miss when they aim." Clamping his lips onto her cheek as if to feed, he simultaneously thrust his foot between my legs until he could push it no further; he wriggled his toes as if squeezing mud between them. Choking, I dropped my glass; Jake caught it, not spilling a drop. "What's the matter, hon?" Thatcher asked, his eyes postcoital as he drew back his foot.

"Went down the wrong way," I said, pressing my legs together, feeling to have given birth to something unwanted. "I'm all right."

Susie stared at me, anxious to convict, keen to execute, no more sympathetic than any judge; my innocence was no less real than any defendant's. "Paranoid," she repeated. "You're the one with the lock on every lid. Always claiming you'll spoon it out next Christmas—"

"I've helped you grasp the intangibles of the situation," he said.

"Imagine what I could do with whatever's in your files." He nodded, saying nothing. "You're so good keeping secrets when you want to. This thing you're sending her off on tomorrow. What is it you want her to look for? What's she going to find? You act like you think you're really onto something."

"Maybe." A feigned guilelessness came naturally to him. "Let's not talk business after work, darlin'—"

"No better time to talk it," she said. "What's this creep got that you want?"

He looked toward the ceiling as he spoke, seeming to visualize something he didn't yet own. "Somebody drops by your house on their way someplace else," he said, "and they go to the bathroom while they're there, and stop up the pipes shittin' gold, you're not going to call a plumber."

She had no response to his homily. Susie had known him from before the beginning, when he and his brother owned nothing but a plane and a field in the Colombian highlands. He admitted to me once that her business acumen brought them to where they were, but only because he had, as he put it, such blind fool timing. I can't imagine she'd ever gotten used to him.

"If there's something you're not telling me, I wish you would," I said, doubting that I would be heard, much less answered. "What've you got me walking into?"

His smile resembled an old incision, a caesarean scar. "If I knew for sure I'd tell you, but I don't. Just take a look and let me know." He raised his glass. "A toast."

"To what?" Susie asked, lifting hers; a waiter refilled it.

"Everything," he said, a whisper to his mother.

Jake held my jacket for me when we rose to leave; I smiled at him, and he grinned in return, his face full of blessings. Gus led us, Jake tailed us; the crowd parted for our movement as if for a clump of bellringing lepers. Everyone in the place must have worked for Dryco, directly or indirectly; reason enough for circumspection. We waited in enveloping night for our cars to arrive. From the west a blur breezed past Thatcher and Gus; a bicycle messenger racing a delivery to one who couldn't wait, each knowing nothing more valuable than a little more time.

"Watch it!" the messenger shouted, flashing by. As he

shot beneath an unbroken streetlight Jake fired. The bicycle passed some distance beyond the light's cone before falling over. Gus put his hand on Jake's shoulder.

"You rushed, Jake," he said. "That's why I didn't act. I could see he was unarmed."

"I'm sorry," said Jake, his knowledge seeming too much for him as he covered his mouth with his hand.

"Remember breath, though. Breathe in as you fire and hold it. Then let it go a few times after." Gus demonstrated. "Like a train. Gets air back into the head."

"Just wing 'em next time, Jake," said Thatcher, dry of emotion. I knew that within he rocked as if in an earthquake. "Low-key. That's the way."

I rode home in a Dryco car to my apartment on King Street, which Dryco also provided; Thatcher gave me many nails that I might use. I lived in the bottom two floors of an 1825 townhouse refitted to postmod standards by the previous occupants. They'd lost it during the Readjustment; maybe they never deserved it, I'd tell myself. Maybe I passed them each morning as they raked at my clothes, calling for pennies, crying for change. On the street and on my stoop were syringes and shards of bottle-glass left by passersby to remind the street's residents how long we'd lingered at our own edges, relying on balance so we wouldn't fall in.

My neighbor on the third floor wasn't screaming. Wrapping my comforter around me when I got into bed as if expecting recovery a thousand years hence, I let my memory squeeze me unconscious. A friend who lived in the neighborhood I'd be visiting told me a story that never made the news. Sixty problem people were shot in Corlears Hook Park by the Army. Sanitation men came in white trucks and buried them in red bags. A woman went to the landfill, after. With bare hands she tore away the earth until she found her husband. Retucking the others beneath their blanket, she carried him off that he might sleep alone. One who watched as she patted the earth down upon his new bed asked where she'd go now. To the grocery, she said, I got mouths to feed.

TWO

• • • •

While waiting at the stoplight we watched tanks roll down First Avenue. In the Readjustment's early months so many control vehicles collapsed through the pavement into the subway that those remaining assigned to Manhattan now only traveled those streets with thicker crusts. A semblance of calm prevailed for the moment in the city's more disgruntled neighborhoods; many within the government, especially Army personnel—some even within Dryco—wished to remove the soldiers from New York as they'd been removed from other cities and send them into Long Island where they were needed. The Drydens said no; the Army couldn't control trouble if it wasn't around to start it.

"It's sad that so many hope for better," said Avi, staring into the one-way glass as if watching his favorite show. "Hope's the truest opium. Better that people work with what they have. But no, they dream that the man on the white donkey will ride up and put everything in its place. As a dream, it's cancer."

"Hasn't cancer a purpose?" I asked, still dreaming that one day I might win an argument with Avi that he admitted to my having won.

"It makes people appreciate the world for what it is," he said.

One tank lagged after the rest, the litter's runt. Had the driver not recognized our car as one of Dryco's own and, for laughs, turned its turret toward us, I don't know what Avi would or could have done. All in Security were able in all fields; Avi, after Gus, was ablest, but I never hoped that he might always save us.

"I've always told you you'd be happier if you took your life for what it is. As would they. It's only karma."

Our car inched eastward on Ninth Street. During the night a cold front swept the clouds from the sky; morning sun glinted off the tears of millions.

"Karma?" I repeated. "*Schmeggege.* You're some Hindu." He smiled, hearing a word from a language he chose to lose. Avi's family were Lubavitcher Hasidim; he left his old world while still in his teens. During his twenties he feasted from faith's buffet, swallowing and passing Unitarianism, Catholicism, Reform Judaism, Buddhism, and more, at last assembling a plate of scraps from which he might thereafter nibble. His unshaken tenet was a belief in an afterlife so redemptive of the life lived before that he saw no greater purpose to his own existence than to relieve others of theirs.

"Take it as a brand name," he said. "Like Kleenex or Lasereo or God. A word you understand without knowing the meaning." He cleaned his glasses with a silk handkerchief his fiancée had given him. "Even media agree," he said, handing me his copy of *Newsweek*. "For the Six Billion," the cover's blurb read, referring to those who'd left our station on the 20th-Century train. I'd scanned the article earlier, finding simple words that presumed to summon understanding from the years during which the perfect Victorian world became our neopost one. Perhaps the editors hoped that unexpected patterns might emerge from what they threw across the pages, but the only pattern these days was the one from which everyone's clothes were cut. There were familiar scenes from the family album; image upon image: Elvis beside Hitler, Joyce next to the Beatles; the sailor kissing the girl in Times Square on V-J Day side-by-side with the burning girl running down the Vietnamese road; Gorbachev's face was shoved between frame 313 of the Zapruder film and the first platoon marching over the Fifty-Ninth Street bridge.

"It seems to me that what we live through are only birth pangs, that the deepest pain awaits after delivery," Avi said. "Who knows? Because ours is a sick world doesn't mean we shouldn't love it."

At the street's far corner was an abandoned Benetton. On its Ninth Street side was a mural limned by locals, showing a line of ill-drawn skeletons wearing gray pinstripes resembling my own, raising metatarsals higher than their skulls in synchronised kick. "Hell's Rockettes," he said. "Terrible perspective."

"They've painted over the numbers along here," our driver said, slowing that we should neither miss the place nor run anyone down.

"It's a few doors west of Avenue A," I said. "That's it."

Excepting the entrance, the building resembled its six-story neighbors, one of a row of cadavers awaiting a new day's lesson. The old tenement architects had often chiseled names above their building's outer doorways, allowing fresh-arrived immigrants a new world dream, that their hovels were not so much less than the Dakota or the Belnord. The steel door of Macaffrey's school was painted chrome yellow; the name above—*Hartman*—gleamed with smudged gilt. The worn faces of stone seraphim poked from twin circles that bookended the word; each circle was formed from three pairs of wings. The angels' eyes poured down their cheeks, as if without suspicion they'd glimpsed this world's Trinity.

"Don't bother them, Avi," I said, referring to those yet unblinded, the ones on the curbs and steps and stoops. Figures I had read claimed that Loisaida's population density approached what it had been at the turn of the previous century, but that didn't seem possible; too many of the old buildings were gone, and the streets could not have lodged so many.

"If it's necessary I act, Joanna. You know that."

The grace of Avi's that doomed and saved was that he understood his own purpose so well. After we emerged the driver locked the car from within; electrified its body for our visit's duration. Dozens at once encircled and separated us, waving empty cups in outstretched hands, their cloud buzzing as might a beehive's.

"Money," they cried. "Please. Money for food. Money."

I allowed my eyes to lose their focus, that it would seem those people were not truly there. Shaking lesioned fingers from my shoulders, I tried to push through. Someone shoved a fist into my pants pocket, restraining me. "You got money, bitch," my assailant said, yanking as if to rip away my clothes; he was too weak to do more than hold me back. His eyes were as dead as an angel's. "Give it to me." I tried to escape but he wouldn't, or couldn't, free his hand.

"Avi," I shouted; he swam toward me through the crowd. "Get him away—"

"*Gimme money*—" Avi's hand encircled the man's neck. I pulled him from my pocket as Avi lowered him to the sidewalk. The crowd dispersed, seeming much calmer. Avi let go, took my arm and led me off.

"You killed him?" I asked, my leg still warm with the man's touch.

He nodded. "Forget." We dashed up the school's worn

stairs. Avi used unarmed methods that shed no blood and therefore left him sinless. Forget? I tried. Though I'd housebroken compassion, I still wet my bed at night.

Once buzzed in we entered a hall that was enlarged to serve as foyer. Posters taped asymmetrically around the walls bandaged the plaster's wounds. Some enumerated medical litanies and the ninety-eight warning signs of cancer. Another gave numbers to call in event of rape, robbery, accident, or suicide, with no assurance of any answer to any question. A third, drawn in garish colors, diagrammed the proper use of contraceptives. One poster was but a photo of kittens sitting among flowers. They looked stuffed. A fiftyish woman sat behind a paint-speckled desk. She had fresh mums in a jar and fresh gauze around her arm.

"We're from Dryco," I said. "We have an appointment to see Lester Macaffrey."

The doctors must have taken her larynx in removing her cancer; when she spoke she lifted a microphone to her throat, her generated voice sounding more mechanical than a Toyota's. "Third floor, second door on the right."

As she returned to her work we began ours, ascending the narrow stairs at the rear of the hall. Former residents, the apartment-dwellers past, left nothing behind but their vegetable tang, the faint odors of cooked lentils, boiled cabbage and, as if we passed a marketstall, a whiff of cilantro. It seemed too quiet to be a school. The drawings of students hung on the walls we passed.

"Good color sense," said Avi. "You expect a thematic repetition, considering their age."

Some of the pictures might have been drawn by any child living in Beirut or Belfast or Johannesburg. Others were identifiable as designs of our neighborhoods. In those, crowds raced from distant buildings that spewed inky clouds, soldiers shot young men in their yards, children ran after wagons carrying off their dogs. An artist of a traditional school sketched a suburban design, unexceptional but for detail: a mother and father stood before their house, holding the hands of half a child. The gallery continued beyond the third floor; we went no further. Hearing at last the sound of children's laughter, I wondered at whom they laughed. On the glass of Macaffrey's door a stenciled message read *Knowledge is Danger*.

"Visitors," called a man's voice when I knocked. "Come on in." Avi slipped ahead of me, opening the door; I saw him, inside. Macaffrey's look was that of a million's; once out of my sight, I couldn't have more accurately described his look than a cloud's. "Sit with the rest or stand in the corner."

Choosing to stand, we noted absentees: there were no desks, no chairs, no books or blackboard, no TV or tape-player. Only half the windows had glass; on this cool day all wore their wraps. The unobservant might have found the pupils no more memorable than their teacher. They must have had homes, for all appeared washed, and if Macaffrey supplied their clothes he must have provided detergent as well. Perhaps he had trouble with shoes; most wore sandals fashioned from strips of tire and rope. A girl sitting in the front row, her hands clasped before her in her lap, spoke to us. The rest of the class was preternaturally still.

"We were—" She halted, and scratched her head, searching for the word she wanted; each of her hands bore an extra thumb. "Discussing, that's it. We were discussing the fall of man." She laughed. "Man's first disobedience. The fruit of that tree."

"You're studying Milton?" I asked.

He looked at me; I stared between his eyes as he spoke, as if I were being interviewed. "Biblical interpretation of every sort has its purpose, you know." Avi and I frowned in unison, as might twins, each of us surely thinking that we had found nothing more than the usual fundamentalist continuing to eat through the woodwork. Scholars suspected that American students would find the legend of creationism no more comprehensible than the theory of evolution, therefore remaining untainted by either, but I had my doubts, and suspected Macaffrey of being one of those keen to demonstrate to the young that the only proper logic is none at all; so I imagined, until he began.

"Let's recap for the benefit of our guests," he said. "The key to understanding the first chapters of Genesis is remembering that nothing in it is written as it happened. What do we call such writing?"

A girl with hair the color of crow's wings lifted her arm, her hand reaching no higher than her head. Another child of that test group; her legs were little more than stubs propping her squat body aright. "Allegorical," she said, her voice raw, sounding as if she'd smoked and drank heavily, awaiting exit from the womb. "Truth bedecked in Halloween drag."

Neither game nor video could have seduced Macaffrey's audience into taking their eyes off the screen he presented. "Good, Marge. So face facts. Seven days represent billions of years. Keep in mind that this was written for people who didn't know from hours. With that ground planted, let's get to the growing. What was that snake, and what made it special?"

"They meant Neanderthal people," said a boy. "Godness liked Neanderthal people. They couldn't talk but they communicated."

"They had flowers at their funerals," added another boy, perfect enough but for the ragged scar transversing each cheek.

"They saw Adam and Eve," said Macaffrey. "Who were they?"

"Cro-Magnon," shouted a girl. I looked and looked again, but saw nothing wrong with her. "God liked them. They acted without a script."

"They yearned to burn," said a boy standing on his

hands; without legs, he waved like wheat in the wind. "No patience."

"There're two kinds of people in the world," said Macaffrey. "The Garden was the world as it once was, as it was intended to be. Everything was very peaceful for a very long time. Both groups kept to themselves. They did as they'd always done. There were no problems. No disruptions. They were very afraid, and didn't know why. What was the matter?"

"They knew they weren't complete," said the girl with four thumbs.

"Their creation, though perfect, wasn't whole. It was divided, as They were. Godness knew that our intermingling would cause no end of trouble but knew as well that the choice would have to lie with us. She put the flea in the serpent's ear—symbolically, of course." The students laughed, as if knowing well the answer to a riddle just heard. "We've known responsibility for our actions ever since."

"So what happened?" Avi asked, as if hearing it for the first time.

"Opposites magnetize," said the crow-haired girl. "Wanting to mindblow, they aimed bedways."

"Cain and Abel were the first children," said a boy, scratching his ear with his toe as he spoke. "They suffered for being first."

"For being human. Their children's children were as us," said Macaffrey. "They know They put too much of Themselves into us and it drives Them crazier than They already are. As we forever throw ourselves off cliffs to see if we can fly, so They forever strive to sort things out, certain that one day an imperfect being will fit into a once-perfect world. They're still learning, too," he concluded. "Class dismissed."

Once undammed the children flooded from the room. Macaffrey remained where he stood as his listeners left, looking to have reached the chopping block and wondering what delayed his executioner. His natural speaking voice was different from his teaching tones, looser yet clipped, and possessed of a heavier twang than Thatcher's.

"I been expecting you," he said, his eyes turning toward ours; I looked away, wishing not to be so quickly lured.

"What on earth are you teaching them?" I asked.

He grinned. "Kind of adapted to circumstance over the years. Only way to get some things across is to lose them in the packaging, you might say. Like putting vitamins in sugar. What're you here for? Come by for private lessons?"

"The head of our company wants—" What did Thatcher want? "Wants to see you tomorrow, in our office."

"There's a reason for this honor?" he asked, his voice sharp with the same edge that Bernard's sometimes bore.

"He seems to believe you might have something to tell him."

Had Bernard not told me Macaffrey's age I could only have guessed it to be somewhere between seventeen and forty, his appearance varied so in the room's shifting light. "Does Macy's tell Sears?" he asked. Did Southerners speak only in riddles? With such responses he and Thatcher might prove made for each other.

"How do you conceptualize?" Avi asked—an unexpected miracle for him to stir from his solipsism long enough to hear a stranger's words. Still, for Avi to grant attention did not assure trust.

"They come to me," he said.

"You've got the sound of a state Christian," said Avi. "Just doing the police in different voices." One night Avi told me about his fiancée. On a morning during the troubles she'd been on a bankline. A gang burst in, members of a sect who frowned upon the sins of moneylenders and their clients. Avi hoped she'd been thinking of him as she died, but I doubted she was. They watched her watch her blood wash the marble pink beneath her. The truth later emerged about poor old Jesus, so conveniently released that it might have been by design, settling the restless, eliminating old troubles that the new ones could crowd in. Those guilty of lesser murders were never punished; during his retreat Avi conceived a readjusted creed, and upon reentering the world came to Dryco as Bernard and I did, our memories of the lost world willfully erased. Amnesia came as easily as hunger, after awhile.

Macaffrey seemed ashamed to be so accused. "My father was a minister who passed out grape juice, lying it was wine." I wondered who I might see staring back at me if I looked into his eyes. "My family knew their purpose. Doesn't matter. You like our school?"

"You have a refreshing approach," I said. "Your students are remarkably articulate for their age—"

"When they want to be, they are," he said. "They saw you staring. It doesn't surprise them or please them."

"I'm sorry," I said. "I've read about them but never seen—"

"Social worker words," he said, smiling. "Sideshow eyes. They're in their own world, after all." He lowered his voice, as if to detail his own conspiracy. "Some of them talked minutes after they were born, you know. Doctor I once knew explained that their vocal cords had already lowered, or risen, or however it works. Generally that's why babies don't talk, but they did. That's not the most wonderful thing—"

"What is?"

"If they knew how to talk when they were born, think how long they must have been listening." His cheeks crushed his eyelids together as he smiled, burying his gaze beneath wrinkles. "Why's your boss want to see me?" he asked, his eyes suddenly open, and I staring into them. When I first tried to speak, I couldn't; finally I stammered a reply.

"If I knew I wouldn't be allowed to say."

"Fair enough," he said. "I'll be there at noon tomorrow, once my classes are done."

"We'll send a car—"

"I'll get there," he said, opening the door. "Let me walk you downstairs, make sure you get out all right."

As he led us away I knew an uneasy comfort, the feeling a beaten child might know if her parent suddenly tossed aside the whip to gather her young one into her arms. Other teachers passed us on our way down, patting Macaffrey's arms and shoulders; students slowed, rushing by. He nodded to all, an incumbent cruising his electorate.

The man's body still lay on the sidewalk. Macaffrey sighed as he saw him. "Your handiwork?" he asked Avi, who murmured admittance, his hand caught in the cookie jar. Kneeling, Macaffrey placed his hand on the man's chest and shook him. He turned his head to look at us, fixing his unblinking eyes upon mine. My knees gave way, for I hadn't fought off his look; I started to slump, and felt Avi's arm encircling my waist, holding me up. The one hitherto lost to the world blinked his eyes.

"Behave!" Lester said, helping the man to his feet. "How old are you, friend?"

He looked sixty. "Eighteen."

"Then you ought to know what can happen when you bother people you don't know. Go on, get out of here. Don't do it again. Go on."

The man stumbled toward Avenue A, patting his head as if trying to remember where he'd had it. Avi and I looked around. Word of Macaffrey's appearances passed quickly; peering from windows, gazing out of doors, poking faces above the roofs of cars, the block's hundreds showed themselves, none speaking, none moving, all watching Macaffrey. He looked back at them with emotions I hadn't allowed myself to feel publicly for years, shivered and spoke.

"Noon tomorrow, then," he said, almost whispering,

rushing back to the yellow door, seeming as haunted by the neighbor's eyes as I was by his.

"You don't know where it is," I said.

"I do."

"Send kids to the circus and all they tell you about are the clowns," said Bernard. We had no more trouble recounting what we'd seen than we would have had explaining it. I felt I should have worn cap and bells during our presentation, so foolish it sounded away from his presence.

"A con," said Susie, certain that we'd failed, certain that she'd predicted as much; by her inerrant prophecy reaffirming her worth. She spread her eyelids with her fingers as if threatening to pop her eyes out at us. "It's all in the peepers. Nothing but psychohypnosis."

"Sounds like he's got the look to me," said Thatcher.

"The Hitler look," said Susie.

"That could be usable, depending on the circumstances—" said Bernard.

"He obviously believes what he says, it sounds like," said Thatcher.

"Then he's even crazier than we imagine," said Susie.

"His messages would seem comprehensible to most nine-year-olds, so you could reach a large enough audience over time," said Bernard. "It's helpful if he does believe what he says, we'll get that unmistakable burp of honesty coming through the more obscure parts of the text—"

"Could he work on mass scale?" Thatcher asked.

Bernard shrugged. "We'd have to run the usual tests. See if he washes. It could be done, perhaps. Religion's simply an aspect of popular culture mutated. Only—"

"We saw what was there," said Avi. "I certified death."

"How can you tell anymore?" Susie asked. "They must all look the same by now." Avi shook his head.

"He look dead to you?" Thatcher asked me.

"I'm no expert," I said. "I thought so."

"Macaffrey could have told you the sun was the moon and you'd've thought so," said Susie.

"It is odd he had you so enthralled and ignored the chance to go all the way," Bernard said. "While you two were fisheyed he didn't pass along idle commentary on the brotherhood of life? No sidebars concerning meaning? A better race?" Bernard wrinkled his nose. "Natural diets?"

"All he talked about was what I've told you," I said.

"Small-bore ammo," said Bernard. "So we have a nondescript who tells Bible stories of his own devising to special children and who, in his spare time, brings muggers back to life." He chewed his thumb as he spoke. "Wouldn't be the easiest sell to any market."

"Let's shelve this for the moment," said Susie. "We have to examine the Jensen situation."

"It's being seen to," said Bernard.

"Boy sounds like he can talk some trash," said Thatcher. "That's good. I need somebody convincing."

"He can't even keep his anthropology straight," said Susie. "Neanderthals. *Goddess*—"

"Godness," Avi corrected.

"Fucking hell—"

"This time tomorrow," Thatcher said, "we'll get ourselves a good look at God. Next best thing, anyhow." Throwing his head back he laughed with the delight of a boy racing through a thunderstorm, unmindful of lightning. He glanced at me, hoping to glimpse my response to this day's invitation. I nodded my head; he could have me, that night. "What a wonderful world," he said, his smile uncharacteristically beatific.

Wishing forgiveness for previous trespasses, Thatcher hadn't entered me for almost a year. He took pleasure rubbing himself raw against me, laying out the scenario desired that I might serve as metteuse-en-scene. "I'll remember you in my will, hon," he always said, after. Though he provided it I never invited him to my place. We met that night at his apartment in the north Trade Tower, a reconverted ninetieth-floor suite. At such altitude drapes were superfluous; moonlight shining through the narrow windows threw bars of shadow across our bed. Tossing aside the sheets, I broke from my prison, walked over and looked out, the moon seeming so close that it could have been part of the decor. Thatcher beat his belly as if it were a drum when he rose, sending his victory cry to all his fellow beasts. His city pieds-à-terre served as warehouses as well, where purchases were stored until the executors might sort them out. From a stack of packages he removed a box, pulling from it what appeared in the dark as some archaeological relic.

"Jim Beam did a lot of figurines," he said, proffering what I realized to be a two-liter bottle in the form of a bejeweled, bloated Elvis. "Wanted one since I saw it in a liquor store, when I was a punk. Two thousand dollars." Two hundred thousand old dollars; with that sum he could have fed a fraction of the starving, once. "He'd have drunk it, if he'd drunk. He did touch the bottle. Got a paper with it authenticated."

I discerned a date stamped on the bottom; I'd only been graduated from Middlebury that year, and believed as I exposed myself to the real world's virus that the country could never be worse off. "He was dead when they made it," I said.

Even when he loved, and he did, in his fashion, Thatcher condescended. "One of these days E'll come again," he said, shaking his head. With worshiping touch he rewrapped his icon within its Mylar winding-sheet. "Jerusalem Slim struck out like all the rest, but E'll turn up at the bottom of the ninth. Wait and see."

"Maybe you can buy him when he shows up," I said.

"Let's make do with what we have, for the moment," he said. "How'd this Macaffrey bird really strike you, hon?"

30

"He's got something," I said. "I'm not sure what. He'll cause trouble doing whatever he does, I'm sure. He seems rather independent—" Thatcher's shoulders shook; he failed to hide his laughter, and I slapped him across the back of his head. He stopped laughing, overcome with emotion. "If you're going to ask for my opinion, would you at least pretend to listen—?"

"I'm not laughin' at you, hon," he said, slipping his arm around me. "It's the concept's got me going. I'm listening. Go on."

"He seems to mean well in what he does. Probably makes him feel less guilty—"

"Guilty?" Thatcher repeated, as if learning the phonics of an unfamiliar word. "Guilty about what?"

"I don't know, most people are—"

"Whose feelings we talking about here?"

"It's how it struck me—"

"You got a crush on him already, don't you?" I ignored him. "That's sweet. He sure had you all convinced of something over there. Never heard such carrying on as when you all got back." Slipping again into shadow, he seemed no more than embodied dark. "Avi doesn't get fired up too easy. And as for you, you've worked with Bernard so long that an awful lot of him's wore off on you. Always bitin' the hand that feeds you. Not enough respect to pour into a thimble. Vipers, that's all you are."

"I'm not like Bernard."

"Bernard's got a different wound than you have—" he started to say.

"Not by much."

"You both got what I need."

As he leaned forward his head reemerged into light, his face reflecting city and moonshine as he kissed me. "What the fuck are you planning, Thatcher?" I said.

"Walls always have ears, hon. Let's keep things general."

"Couldn't get less specific."

31

"Say somebody came along that seemed to be the messiah," he said. "Seemed that way often enough to enough people, at least."

"What sort of messiah?"

"How many kinds are there?" he asked. "I don't mean palm readers, no gypsies reading tea leaves. No California babes talking about Egypt or Atlantis or Mars. I mean the real McCoy. What if you caught him in the wings while he was waiting to go onstage?" His eyes held the light, shining like beacons, cleaving the dark. "How would you effect a co-opt? Could you interface him into the corporate frame? How much weight could he throw in the marketplace?"

"What if he's not—"

He lifted his arms, seeming to catch one tumbling to earth. "Making a tree grow fruit in the wilderness. That's business, plain and simple."

Hearing screams, I remained mute, not having to convince myself that my actions could prevent a crime. "You're crazy, Thatcher."

"Say he isn't anything but a good talker with the look, like Susie thinks," said Thatcher. "So? Doesn't mean he can't get things done with our help. She's good with the details but she can be blind as a bat with the big picture. If the idea's too—what's the word I want—"

"Crazy."

"Transcendent," he said. "With a little coaching, fellow like Macaffrey could do us a world of good. Show him which side of bread to put the butter on. How to slice up the loaf."

"Why do you want a messiah?" I asked. "Why?"

"It's not like it hasn't been done before," he said, ignoring me as well as if I were but another lost in the surrounding crowd, one whose words went unheard, whose existence was as inessential as fog. "Tell people somebody's something often enough and everybody comes around to believe it in time."

I could never be such a devil's advocate as Bernard, but I had my moments. "What if he is the messiah?" I asked. "What then?"

Thatcher walked across the room to look over his land, staring into Long Island's crimson air. Retrieving my clothes I began to dress, wondering if in his reverie he could even see me. He kept the air conditioning so high in his rooms that my soul felt chilled; I shivered, feeling as might a traveler lost in a blizzard, collapsing into a drift, ignoring all coming down around me, overcome by entombing cold, allowing my eyes to shut slowly beneath the weight of the snow.

"Different runway," he said. "Same approach." He turned to watch me zip my skirt. "Heathen might just get what they want for a change, or what they think they want."

Heathern, the word emerged, mangled by his accent. All were heathern in his eyes; had they become so in mine as well? A heathern world deserved a heathern messiah, yes, but what of our world, our sick world, our wonderful world? Which did it less deserve, its creators or its keepers?

THREE

······

In morning's more transcendent glow we awaited Macaffrey, thinking or speaking of anything else. "We examined Jensen's office files," said Gus, lifting a sheet of paper. "With police I searched his apartment in the Bronx, and his sister's in Chelsea. They found it in her place."

"Did she know it was there?" Thatcher asked, reclining in his chair, gazing through the wall-wide window onto 40 Wall Tower's pyramid crown and the ocean beyond. Sparrows and gulls flew by, uncaring of Dryco actions. Susie took shelter beneath her paper's tent.

"Our silence was so effective that she was unaware of her brother's death until we told her. Interrogations proceed without result."

"Cat's got her tongue," said Bernard.

"Let's see what you got," said Thatcher. Looking over his

shoulder, I read what was written, seeing carefully inscribed black letters: MAHAICA *Conrad Taylor* MYSTIC *Mitch Moseley 3 days 25 percent.* Susie declined to examine the note. "What the hell's it mean?"

"As it has no evident meaning it must be pertinent," said Gus. "Mahaica is the name of a small port southeast of Georgetown, Guyana. No other references to this name exist in the files. What remains appears to be shorthand rather than code. In either event, the names, the figures, the word *mystic*, the meaning of those is still unclear."

"Guyana?" Thatcher repeated. "Jim Jones territory?" Bernard nodded. "Nobody wants him, he's dead. What else's Guyana got?"

"The usual raw materials," said Bernard. "It's an inessential state, except perhaps to Guyanans. No information received suggests Japanese interests presently operating in Guyana."

"No evident interests," said Thatcher. One night while I was with him he drank to excess and began rambling about hiring Godzilla to destabilize Japan. I had to have Avi put him to bed before I went home. "They've been taking all this time figuring out how to get into it right. Cut their losses before they even begin—"

"Who wrote this note?" asked Susie, tossing aside her paper as she might a kitten she'd tired of petting. "Jensen?"

Gus shook his head. "No ID thus far. The lettering is done with felttip pen such as any criminal might use."

"What's the provenance of the paper?" Bernard asked.

"Standard notepad with a difference," said Gus, holding it against the light that we might see the watermark's modification, the fang protruding from the empty face's smirk on our company's happy-face logo. Bernard designed both versions of the trademark, the open and the closed. "The paper came from this floor."

"Jensen ever come up here?" Thatcher asked.

"Never," said Gus. "The guard wouldn't have accessed him."

"So either he came in with somebody, or somebody was already here doing his business for him. Who's allowed on this floor?"

"Many," said Gus. "Politicians, Army representatives, publishers, your friends, company executives, government officials—"

"Charwomen, maintenants, anyone in the upper three levels of Security," said Susie.

"Messiahs," said Bernard.

"We can clear most of those," said Thatcher, "There's still a rat in the cheese factory. Whoever's behind this is using our people. Who among us is most corruptible?"

"Blessings are equal, all around," said Bernard. "The Army, perhaps. There're enough of them around here, you'd think it was a VFW hall—"

"It's not the Army," said Thatcher.

"If he had Latin American dealings he would have liaisoned with Army personnel at times," said Susie. "Any reports of renegade elements within the ranks? Conceivably he was contacted—"

"Reports from all fields are analyzed by sociopathologists for disturbing motifs recurring in the subtext," Bernard said. "That way those bent twigs may be swiftly pruned. They're examined for signs of the boys enjoying themselves too much, or for patterns of fatalism, signs of disagreement with stated policies, the usual things. The prizewinners this year were a group of pilots who were flying copters into central Jersey at night to land in fields and mutilate farm animals." He laughed. "Those guys. Amateur devil worshippers off on a toot."

"What happened to them?"

"Transferred to the Turkish theater," said Bernard. "Busy mutilating Turks now, I suppose."

"If Jensen couldn't get in up here no one in the Army ranks could have helped him access, whether they were in or out," I said. "Army involvement would assume knowledge on the part of some in Command, wouldn't it? Who analyzes their reports?"

Bernard shrugged. "Quis custodiet ipsos custodes?"

Thatcher spoke again, ignoring Bernard's sudden lapse into tongues. "The Army's not in this, I tell you," he said. "They see things different than we do, that's all. They may not be too grateful but they don't forget who kept 'em going when times was hard."

"Why would Frankenstein mind being given a gun?" asked Bernard.

"Let's be realistic," said Thatcher. "You and I know who we're looking for—"

"While it's possible the Japanese are involved, I'm sure it would be only coincidentally. They've had so little involvement in the area in the past—"

"Think there's a possibility, though?"

"Anything's *possible*, Thatcher," Bernard said. "We still have to get this agreement signed, whether they're involved or not. After that our problems are over, wherever they arise."

"Over?" Susie asked. "Done?"

Thatcher nodded. "You say this guy's into a lot of things—"

"So many that conceivably a renegade within his organization might possibly be in on this. As, possibly, ones of ours have been involved. But he probably isn't the one immediately behind it. The Japanese aren't crazy—"

"They play golf on top of skyscrapers," Thatcher said, speaking slowly, as if to children. "Keep robot fish in their aquariums. Put fresh air in spray cans. Watch movies of little girls killing each other with swords—"

"So they're crazy as Americans," said Bernard.

"They got fifth columnists in half my businesses and I can't fire the bastards, they're too good. They're trying to get me in bad with the government."

"Aren't you constantly telling me not to worry about the government?"

"It's not as cut and dried as I'd like it to be," said Thatcher. "You all act like we're already the government, but you can't hurry love. That's why things still have to look halfway right. We'll always have to have elections, for example, there's no getting around it—"

"Subtleties," said Susie, "or so you always say."

"You're safe as milk, Thatcher," said Bernard. "The populace has stayed so sober since it broke that terrible addiction to truth."

"Never know what might get leaked," said Thatcher. "To the media."

"Even the media you don't own want nothing to do with unlocking your closet," said Bernard. "More pressing problems need attention. The scams of beggars. Serial killers in the ranks of environmentalists. Subliminal messages on cereal boxes within the pictures of missing children. Keep in mind, all we have to do ninety-nine times out of a hundred is put the cap over the lens. Then there is no situation."

"Mister Dryden," Lilly called over the intercom. It was noon. "Lester Macaffrey to see you."

"Send him in," said Thatcher. "Never enough time to do everything that needs doing. All right, Gus, stay on Jensen's trail. Give Macaffrey a rubdown, too, why don't you?"

As the door slid open Gus walked over and patted Macaffrey's limbs, as if to flour him. "Three times for luck?" Macaffrey asked, his arms outstretched. "Or ritual?"

"Precautions," said Thatcher. "Have a seat. Good of you to come see us on such short notice. Never heard such good things about a teacher before, Lester."

"Mister Macaffrey will do for now," he said, sitting down. "You understand."

Avi had been invited to the meeting; when I asked if he was coming he shook his head, and walked away. I always knew when he was scared, even if he didn't. "Nice offices you got here. I'm surprised it's not the penthouse."

"Precautions," Thatcher reiterated. A question of blast direction, Avi told me; the roof blew up if anything heavier than a pigeon landed upon it, destroying as well the floor immediately below, the observation deck. "Mister Macaffrey, then. What I've heard about you makes me think your talents might be going to seed. I'd like to offer you a bigger field to sow."

Macaffrey's stare seemed not so withering as it had the day before; I wondered if his mesmerism's effect could be likened to that of a drug to which one became addicted without ever feeling the high. Susie slipped on sunglasses, looking as a gorgon lifting her own mirrors against those who came to harm her.

"Maybe you've heard of Dryco," said Thatcher. "We keep a low profile, but we're into more things than you could shake a stick at. What we lack is consistency. Got lots of material and no grand design. No theory."

"You need a moral outline," said Macaffrey. "How could a teacher teach that?"

"For a teacher your educational record is refreshingly free of degree," said Bernard, reading his printout. "We have no evidence that you were even graduated from high school. How did you come into your present position?"

"Fell into it," he said. "Neighborhood folks saw me as a natural, I suppose. I don't think the Board of Regents minds my taking my students off their hands."

"Yesterday you said your father was a minister," said Susie. As she sat there, her eyes unreadable behind those shades, she seemed only to lack a cup filled with pencils. "Of what breed? Something respectable? Fundamentalist? Racialist? Any interest in politics? How much experience has your family had in this area?"

"Were the standard old ladies fleeced?" asked Bernard. "Did he molest innocent minds? Could he convince his flock that hell was worse than what they had?"

Macaffrey answered, his face totemic, showing nothing, holding all. "My father was an Episcopal priest. He found good in unlikely places. I think he was happy with his life. In the fall he blessed the foxhounds before the hunts began."

Bernard winked. "Who blessed the fox?"

"Is this a genealogical society?" Macaffrey asked. "I don't understand what my family has to do with this—"

"Background checks. Precautions," said Thatcher. "Looking for the man behind the mask. It's easy to lose the human element in all this if you're not careful."

"Heaven forbid," said Bernard. "Much of a churchgoer yourself, Lester? Not much point these days, is there?"

"I'm no joiner."

"In our service economy," said Bernard, "who do you serve? God?"

"No less than anyone."

Bernard loved a challenge—to a point—and responded at full tilt. "I wish my teachers had been so creative. Such invention you have. Way above the norm, I assure you. It's tricky, you know, to describe a creative act without tossing the Lord in somewhere, I suppose, but I find such vagueness unholy. I'm told these concepts of yours came to you. How? In dreams? A bottle? Do you file through some heavenly fax? Do you consider your truth to be true?"

"I've said it long enough that I should." Bernard's net was ready but the butterfly wouldn't settle. More familiar with Thatcher's logic, Bernard reconsidered, and readied the killing jar.

"Good man in procurement, we hear," he said. "What's involved in that? You look up in the sky until you see what's falling? Some geyser of bounty shoots up between your feet? Where do you come by your gifts?"

"Everybody has connections," said Macaffrey. "No mystery in that."

"Tricks are fine for television but we have no cameras here." Thatcher once told me that there were twelve in the room. "Some here in our audience gave boffo reviews for your act's finale. Can you raise the dead?"

"To be what?" Bernard pursed his lips and looked down at his printout.

"Maybe you're not taking this in the right way," said Thatcher, leaving it purposefully unclear as to whom he spoke. "Mister Macaffrey. If Gus was to throw you through that window, would you fall?"

"Under the circumstances you'd risk it?"

"I wouldn't be putting in an investment to lose, if you fell. You get used to taking risks in business like you get used to breathing, you know. It seems to me that there's mighty big stuff being hinted at here and I'd like to see something more impressive. I want to know if you're all you say you are."

"I'm nothing," said Macaffrey. "I'm here at your request. If you're so sure of what you see, why should I give you glasses?"

"Gus," said Thatcher, "go out in the hall, bring Jake in here a minute."

"Why?"

"I won't hurt him." Gus went to retrieve, and the dialogue continued.

"Is there something you're planning?" asked Macaffrey.

"You're probably aware that most everybody in your line claims some degree of medical skill," said Thatcher. "None of 'em ever come saying they're a psychic accountant, for example. Guess God never has to balance His own books."

"I'm no doctor."

"Bringin' somebody back to life's damn good doctoring, long as they were dead," said Thatcher. "Course if you can do that we have a new problem, deciding who to keep—"

Gus returned with his protégé. Jake stood silently, awaiting his orders, clasping his hands over his groin.

"You been working over a year for us now, right?" asked Thatcher.

Jake nodded. I don't believe he'd ever been in the boardroom before.

"You've done a good job for us. Good potential. You don't fuck around, Jake."

"I sting the bees." With quick fingers Jake smoothed his clothes, an unconstructed white jacket and ironed jeans.

"That's the way God planned it. I hear you never let on when it hurts."

"Not overmuch, nada nohow."

"What does hurt you?"

"Tooth Nazis," he said.

"No root canal this trip," said Thatcher. "You don't mind blood tests, do you? How often you get those?"

"Bimonthed as required."

"Think of this as a blood test," said Thatcher. "Jake, Gus is going to break one of your fingers and then we'll see if this boy can fix you up. You pick the finger."

After a moment's hesitation Jake lifted his left arm, extending a pinky no larger than my own.

"There's a purpose to this, Mister Dryden?" Gus asked.

"Told you I wasn't going to hurt him," said Thatcher, smiling. "Get to it, Gus, don't have all day."

Gus broke bones with the greatest finesse, I was told; even so, I closed my eyes and covered my ears. Looking again I saw Jake motionless, as a statue of smooth cold marble. His arm was pressed against his side; his finger jutted away from his hand at an unnatural angle.

"What do you suggest?" Thatcher asked Macaffrey. Macaffrey's look held no threat of trance.

"Take him to the hospital," he said. "He'll go into shock."

"You don't think you can fix it?" asked Thatcher.

"I always fail tests."

"But you passed, son. If you'd tried faking it you'd've already hit the street. Jake, that hurt much?"

Jake's lips barely moved. "No."

"AOK then. Gus, take him to the clinic." Jake shook Gus's hand from his shoulder as they walked away. Bernard tapped his pencil against the tabletop. Susie's eyes were unreadable behind her sunglasses. I tried convincing myself that I wasn't fully there.

"You're everything I've heard, Mister Dryden," said Macaffrey, standing. "I'll be on my way."

"I understand gut reactions," said Thatcher. "Sit back down. I want you to see how valuable you could be to my organization. Sit down."

"What good could I do?" Macaffrey asked.

"You got to have more self-confidence than that. Haven't you once stopped to think what you could be painting if you had a bigger brush?"

"What do you want from me?"

"People always want more than what those who have can give," said Thatcher, seeing no paradox. "But it's gotten to the point where we can't let expectations get much lower—"

"How could they?" asked Bernard.

"Time's come to raise a few hopes. We need to give 'em inspiration. Help 'em get out of bed in the morning. Help us keep a lid on things when the situation warrants it. Main thing we can't forget is that we couldn't do what we do without people."

"You want me to pass out the Kool-Aid," said Macaffrey.

"I hope you're not making unwarranted references," said Thatcher, a century's sorrow soaking his voice at command. "Unfair lies, that's what you've probably heard. Makes me sick to think that's what's still believed." He calmed as he took comfort in truth. "Not ten percent of our money comes from drugs anymore, and we're in the process of phasing that out. We've diversified into a number of fields."

43

"In a number of places."

"It's so easy to go global these days," said Thatcher. "Only limit is how far you can see. Think of it, son. Hundreds of millions of people everywhere and every one of them listening to you. You can give peace to troubled minds. Help groups settle their differences. Solve the problems of tomorrow today. Get that camera in front of you and a few satellites and it's all yours—"

"Thatcher," Bernard said, interrupting, "don't overstate—"

"Think of what things might be like today if TV'd been invented twenty years earlier."

"Television has great power to confound and distract," said Macaffrey. "It saps the soul. I have no desire for unnatural congress."

"Most people'd kill and eat their grandmothers to get on TV," said Thatcher. "Worse, even. We'll start you at six thou per year and see how it goes. No more having to preach to gimpy kids from Farmingdale, that's for sure." Bernard and Susie looked no less stricken than I must have appeared; I made two per year, and Bernard not that much more. "Appropriate raises with suitable results. Fair and equitable. We scratch your back, you scratch ours. Everybody comes out ahead."

"You want me to make people render unto Caesar what Caesar already has," said Macaffrey. "Not much point in that, Mister Dryden. I'm sure you'll get along fine without me." Turning, Macaffrey went to the door, and left.

"What's this?" Thatcher said, watching him leave.

"I think he's saying no," said Bernard.

Susie laughed, flushing so with color that I thought her happiness might kill her. "Found a smart one for a change," she said.

"Thinks he is," said Thatcher. Having seen his seduction foiled, he appeared now to be toying with fantasies of rape.

"He obviously doesn't want to be bothered," I said.

"Leave him alone. Hire an actor for your plots. Weren't you telling me how well that's worked before?"

"Thatcher obviously feels he needs this kernel of winsome sincerity," Bernard said, "to grow his new crop of threats."

"You can't get an actor for this kind of gig," said Thatcher. "Be like a white boy singing the blues. We'll play it by ear. I got a hunch he'll come around when he gets the right prompting." As he turned to me he paused, as if to make me more aware of how soon I would learn of my expanded role in this drama.

Susie spoke to her husband as she got up to leave. "I'm going to the infirmary to check on Jake. Did you have to make Gus do that?"

"It's what we pay 'em for."

That afternoon I stopped by Bernard's office, suspecting I'd never see Macaffrey again, finding it impossible to remove him from my mind. Bernard sat surrounded by remnants of his personality: a photo of his wife, a Clio award he used as a paperweight, a pencil sketch of their late son, who was in a coma for a year before he died. Bernard, maker of millions—old millions—was bankrupt when he signed on at Dryco; I still had my jewelry. In the center of his desk was a brass-colored pen and pencil set in the shape of Dealey Plaza.

"You're here to see our newest commercial," he said as I entered.

"Am I?"

"Sweetness, overseeing new projects requires that you feign interest even in the inanimate ones. Here we go."

His set was a flat screen on the far wall; pressing the remote he rolled the spot, which not so much played as ricocheted. Sequential images flashed on during the first twenty seconds, coming too quick to grasp individually but showing myriad aspects of the worst of our world; the music backgrounding was the orchestral run swelling along the scale as it led to the bridge in "A Day in the Life." Before the mind overloaded the sound and picture changed, the music segued into a full chorus singing the "Song of Joy" from Beethoven's Ninth; the blurs vanished into clean clouds seen at angel's altitude, the light aglow in bright blue air, sunrays lending that Nuremberg touch. As the company's motto superimposed itself onto the clouds it seemed to rise from the depths of heaven.

D R Y C O
Worry not. Wonder not.

"Does it mean anything?" I asked, feeling as if a grenade had gone off in my head.

"Does the signifier need the sign? It's meaning-packed at the core level. We've entered it for several awards—"

"It's unreal even for television, Bernard."

He pulled clippings from a folder on his desk. "Unreal," he said. "Listen to what we have here. Elvis appears on Mexican woman's taco, hundreds come to be healed. Pregnant by alien, woman sues NASA. Teacher at Dartmouth divides polisci class into Gestapo and Jews to illustrate the limits of power—three dead. All of this is just from last week's *Times*. What's the second leading cause of death among white American teenagers?"

"Boredom?"

"Peripherally," he said. "Autoerotic asphyxiation." Men tapped into inexhaustible strength so long as they possessed a battery of irrelevant facts; Bernard owned more than I could count. Men had a way of using their facts to propel them toward imagination, and not to truth. "You couldn't make it up."

"I need to talk to you," I said.

"Work-related?" he asked, shutting off the set.

"Coincidentally."

"Pity," he sighed. "This involves Thatcher's new avatar? At least it keeps him distracted—"

"I've never seen anyone get under your skin so."

"Half-baked Jesus freak," said Bernard. "Too stupid to lie."

"You hate him because you couldn't outtalk him," I said. "It's so obvious." Bernard's mood was changeable as tropical weather, and when he glared I feared I'd roused a typhoon. He didn't blow; the moment passed. "Bernard, what if you'd gotten so sick of working here you couldn't look at yourself in the morning?"

"Where are the mirrors?" he asked, with mimic gestures delineating the room.

"I've got to get away from this," I said. "I spend all my time doing nothing. I see no one but him. It's driving me crazy."

"A benefit of the position," he said. Bernard never responded as I might have preferred, but unlike all others he always listened. "You arrived at any preliminary decisions yet? Been examining options? What have you done besides complain?"

"Avi thinks I should live with my reality."

"Gets tricky after awhile, doesn't it? Jobs, people, fish, all rot after three days. Say you quit. What happens?"

"No income. I lose my apartment. I'm out on the street."

He nodded. "If you get yourself fired?"

"The same."

"If you find another job and then quit?" Bernard asked. "Shouldn't leave one job until you have another one lined up, you know."

"I'd still be working for him."

"What if you request a horizontal promotion?" he asked. "Not in the sense with which you're most recently familiar—"

"Transferred where?" I asked. "Data? I'd be blind in a month."

"You could always go on Workfare," said Bernard. "Enter a shelter. One way or the other, you wouldn't be there long."

"People get by with less than I have—"

"People eat their dead in Brooklyn," he said. "Thatcher's not the worst man I've known. It's bound to happen eventually, so you should enjoy yourself while you can—"

"Some mornings I wake up and just want to run away," I said. "Anywhere. Get in a car and drive and keep on driving."

"Through our great and good land?" His face brightened as if he'd already received his awards. "You've flown over it, sweetness. I've been there. You think New York's bad? The people alone'd give you the willies. They smile the whole time they're bringing the axe down."

"Something's happening to me, Bernard," I said. "I don't know what. It's as if somebody else is running away with me—"

"You're getting older," he said; Bernard always listened, not always intelligently. "Avi's a sensible sort on occasion. Pay attention to what he tells you. Ignore the worst and do your job well. Forget the day as it passes. Enjoy your life as it is."

"That makes me no better than they are," I said. "Worse, because I don't feel as they do."

"Maybe you do and don't want to face it," he said. "These things sneak up on you, you know. Get that look off your face, sweetness, you wanted inspiration? I'm no messiah. I can't tell a crystal from a crack vial." He read his appointment book, his glasses low on his nose. "Pity me, my angel, I have to roll in the gutter with the mayor tonight. He's demanding specific dates as to when the Army might be expected to pacify Queens and I have to leave the date as being sometime during the twenty-first century. He's been causing so much annoyance of late."

"You see no other options for me?"

"See any mirrors?"

"Travelready?" Jake asked, appearing at my office door as I prepared to leave. It was after eight.

"All set," I said. Whenever I left late, alone, Jake assured my safety. Somehow I intimidated him; though never loquacious, he seemed especially numbtongued around me. Jake's was a prodigal's soul; his divine talents so influenced his every action and word as to overwhelm any would-be friend. I noticed a volume of Shakespeare, rather than the expected truncheon, stuffed into his jacket pocket.

"Gus teaches you literature?" I asked as we rode down.

"AO," he said. "Litcrit twicecovered this month."

"So many wonderful characters," I said. Jake's presence aroused in me a deeply buried instinct that was still conceivably maternal. "You have any favorites?"

"Ariel."

A car waited at the curb to carry me home. Before we reached it I heard my name called; there was no forgetting Macaffrey's voice. He walked toward us, across our building's plaza; Jake, recognizing him, allowed him to get to us.

"You haven't been out here all day?" I asked.

"I came back." In the streetlight his face held a hundred years' lines. "Would you walk with me?"

Run was what I wanted to do. "Yes," I said, hearing a stranger speak for me. "Jake, I'll be going a different way tonight. I'll see you Monday."

Jake remained where he stood, cautious as a cat. For the first time I noticed the bone-white cast gloving his finger and, suggesting no medical purpose, the scalpel attached to the tip.

"Tell the driver to go on, Jake," I said. "I'll be all right."

"You're chancing," he said, his sea-changing voice sometimes soprano, sometimes tenor, this moment unexpectedly

49

clear and deep. Jake had only turned fourteen. "You know who lights the lights."

"Worry not," I said, cheerfully corporate. "Have a good weekend."

When we walked away there came an instant of silence, and then he cried out in higher pitch, perhaps only making sure that I still heard him. "Joanna—"

"Jake?" That must have pleased him; without responding, he went inside to go home.

With Macaffrey I wandered down Broad Street's gully. Small buildings plugged the rifts in the range, seeming no more than pebbles eroded from the sides of their mother boulders. Billboards of two years' vintage or older stood atop their low roofs. One sold the winner of the most recent Presidential election, and his face faded a little more each time I passed. Vice President once, he was shot before the last day of March, not more than a month and a half beyond his inauguration. His Vice President died five weeks after being sworn in, when Air Force One collided with a sightseeing helicopter over old Shea Stadium. His successor, dumb old Charlie, tried to escape on the day of the crash; after the jets forced his plane to the ground the crowd awaiting, seeing at last a reason to vote, affirmed that he be soundly beaten in their election. His successor and Thatcher worked something out that suited the Drydens for three months; Gus settled matters in Seattle. The present President, the fifth to take office that year, appreciated whose butter smeared his bread.

"You'd never guess what your company does from the name," said Macaffrey. "What do you do for them?"

"Less and less," I said. "Nominally I oversee new projects."

"Like me?" he asked. "You must stay busy. They get that little fellow fixed up all right? I don't think he looked too kindly on your going off with me."

"Jake takes his job seriously," I said. "Gus took him in off

50

the street as an apprentice a year ago. He's grateful. Why were you out there waiting?"

"Nowhere else to go," he said.

"I'd think your schedule'd be booked—"

"On the way back this afternoon I stopped to get something to eat. When I got back to the school it'd been closed by order of the Army as a disorderly house. It's a subtle approach, I'll admit."

We stood there for a moment as I estimated what I'd done. So many wings, so many flies, and my hands so hard at my work that I wondered if I still knew, at all times, what they did. "I'm so sorry," I said. "Thatcher thinks he can bully anyone into doing what he wants."

"He can," said Macaffrey. "I suppose he thinks he wants me."

"So you've reconsidered," I said. "Well, what choice you got. They've left for the weekend, but I can get them, explain you came back to see—"

"To see you," he said. I hoped I wasn't blushing, but my skin reddens even when someone calls me by my first name. Craning my head, I looked at anything but Macaffrey. When I was young and visited the city with my parents, I remembered how I could look down any of the cross streets and see a river; I glanced into an alley-wide street whose vista was not of water, but the wall of a riverside tower resembling twenty thousand elevator buttons stacked one atop the other.

"Why?"

"We have a mutual interest."

Thus far he differed from other men I'd known only in that he apparently believed what he said at all times, and not solely when it was convenient. "I am sorry you lost your job. Those poor children—"

"They'll be all right," he said. "My job's just starting." A trace of disappointment in his voice made me aware of his sorrow; his sadness over not having yet been able to hook

51

me, I thought it. The street we traveled ended at the island's toe. Battery Park's old trees were cut down by the Army so that mortars might be strategically aimed in the event Long Islanders attacked by sea. The floodwall started rising soon after, and now the guns pointed directly at downtown's only defense against the water. Sirens' sound echoed across the ocean air; damp salt breezes wafted over the wall, bearing dry leaves from trees far afield, their currents rich with smells of rain and oil and dead fish.

"What do you mean?" I asked. "Your job at Dryco?"

"I'll help you see what I mean," he said, lifting his arm before me as if to restrain me from flying away too soon. "Take my hand."

There it was: the sly valentine hand-drawn in crayon, the first shake of the buck's antlers, the molester's unwrapping of the lollipop. Southerners wasted no time, I thought, recalling Thatcher's unctuous chivalry during our first month together, before events slid my being from his mind's upper slot. Men behaved so perfectly until their attention spans failed them.

"Why?"

"To see something pretty." Pressing my hand into his, I marveled at how willfully I fell into any new trap. Then, as if in brownout, all city light dimmed, outshone by the sky as it unexpectedly took fire. Over upper New York harbor no spires or towers disrupt the view of heaven's bowl; I stared freely into its millions from below, gazing up into the crowd as if into a tornado, a mandala, a spiral of DNA. In the midst of the angels' hurricane was an eye of blinding white light. I heard the angels' sight, saw their music as a sound like the roar of the sea in a shell. In knowing their movements I looked into the painful light for so long that I thought my own eyes might melt, but I couldn't turn away.

"They figure it's what we'd expect," he said. "I'm sure it's different in reality. Sometimes you'll hear music, too. They like Wagner."

I let go his hand; the vision faded as it came. The street's chiaroscuro reappeared beneath New York's sky, free once more of angels as it was forever free of oxygen, or stars. Others passing along their nightly circuits appeared to have seen no more than the sidewalk lying before their shoes; New Yorkers looked up only to see what might be falling toward them. Looking at Macaffrey, I thought I'd never felt so secure in my fear. "Call me Lester, Joanna," he said. "I don't hold much with labels."

FOUR
· · · · ·

"You'll see me home?" I asked, knowing he'd agree. A million words raced around our silence as we sailed uptown between Broadway's palisades. In our day the thumbrule was that bony lies became truth rich and strange if the need for belief was great enough. A child might rub her stuffed animals bald, trying to wish them into life; what if she started with a sleeping pet? Reality was never so flexible in fact as in theory. Angels, I told myself: there could have been nothing to see; all was but a blend of sky and delusion.

Closing my eyes, I still saw angels. Why was I chosen to receive revelation? It made as little sense as those stories of flying saucers landing on lonely Nebraska prairies, desiring that farm girls alone should know the secrets between stars. That I liked being with Lester held nothing of heaven.

"That fellow you came to the school with," he said. "You were lovers once?" From distant Brooklyn came the sound of bundled papers being thrown onto a newstand's curb, the nightly cannonade. No doubt I'd opened my mind wide enough that Lester might now easily slip himself in.

"You couldn't know that—"

"It's in the way you stood next to him," he said. "The tilt of your pelvis. It's all in the details. Let's go this way."

We headed west down Rector Street; Trinity Church's encircling boneyard was on our right, bright beneath floodlamp glare; arcs hung from the trees, appearing as fruit passed over at harvest time. The yard's retaining wall rose higher as the street sloped toward the unseeable Hudson River. Turning north again we passed beneath a slender wrought-iron bridge arching above the street, running from the cemetery to an office building, as if the sextons, foreseeing Doomsday, provided for the dead a short walk between grave and Workfare office.

"You broke up with him awhile back?" Lester asked.

"It was a work relationship. We got overinvolved. Not long after we started there. Our jobs got in the way. His job."

"What happened?"

"We had this awful conversation one night," I said. "I called him a golem. Worse than that. We kept talking and stayed friends, but the moment passed." Midtown's distant lights enflamed Manhattan's sky until it appeared no less bloody than Long Island's. The breath of the underworld rose through cracks in the pavement. The Trade Towers stood on our left beyond a low wall of outbuildings. Soldiers guarding the plaza searched and taunted a man delivering pizzas; a lateworker's dinner always arrived cold. "Why am I telling you this?"

"I asked," he said. "Seems so quiet down here at night. Like the old days. Army's really necessary still?"

"Seen as necessary," I said. "Thatcher gets nervous unless he's surrounded."

"Except when he's with you?" Lester asked, no trace of

malice in his question. By moving farther from him, I thought, I could keep him from driving deeper into my mind, deliberately forgetting that I walked with one who showed me God's lack of face.

"Please stop," I said.

"I read people well," he said. "I wish I was illiterate."

"It's as if you've had me investigated," I said. "Watching me come and go and I never knew it. It's an awful feeling—"

"Do you hate me as much as you hate him?" A third pair of feet paused, a second after ours, the sound adding a grace note to our chord. A soldier, I thought, seeing no one; a worker, some clerk leaving a store. A nominal curfew was on; as a Dryco exec I could have probably stepped to the curb and hailed a tank, had I wanted. We continued uptown through ever-darker streets. Helicopters flew over, thrashing the city with sticks of light, searching out those with whom they refused to share hegemony. Wind glued newspapers to our ankles as we walked, losing the day's words.

"I'm sorry," he said. "It's too easy to see what people think."

"But you have to tell them?" I said. "People don't have enough to worry about without strangers raping their minds?"

"People never worry about what they should," he said, "and so often rape happens with someone you thought you loved. You wouldn't trust me if I weren't a stranger."

"Don't they hate you for this in your neighborhood?" I asked. "Reminding people of what they want to forget?"

"It's a sin to see wrong and do nothing about it."

"So God's the greatest sinner?" I asked, the Bernard in my soul leaping forth.

"Yes and no," he said. We passed an old post office recycled years ago into a Health Service clinic. A long line of silent people awaited entry into the waiting room. Brass railings green with verdigris guarded its graffitied walls. A sign affixed to the granite tallied late additions to the six billion.

"Even They have to make the best of what They've made," he continued. "Does it make sense that in a better world this would be a better world?"

I wondered what might be expected of God-Godness if Their apparent messenger could sound so transcendent. "You see what you showed me all the time or only if you want to?"

"How else?" he asked, laughing. A wild wind, an angel's breath, swept his hair across his forehead, for a moment taking twenty years from his look. "I've learned to live with what comes to me."

"Can you see the future?"

"Can't you?" he asked, sweeping his arm out before us. The familiar whoop of an oncoming siren sounded as an infant's wail. Facing the street, we lifted our arms above our heads. The mayor's limo rolled uptown, surrounded by motorcycle cops, preceded and followed by flatbed trucks carrying soldiers thrusting their rifles forth in every direction, pins in pincushions.

"He never visits my neighborhood," he said. "When they pass I'm always tempted to keep walking as the hearing-impaired do—"

"You'd be shot as they're always shot," I said.

"Considering how he treats the innocent, how does your Mister Dryden deal with the guilty?"

"Depends on who's guilty of what," I said. "He never gets his own hands dirty." My earlier question returned to mind. "You never said if you could see the future. Can you?"

"Some people's futures," he said.

"Whose?"

"Mine," he said. "Yours."

Reaching the corner of Duane Street South we stopped for the light; someone else stopped. There was nothing Thatcher had taught me so well as the acceptance of fear's comfort. Seeing no one, I knew they were there.

"We're being followed," I said.

"No, we're not—"

"Listen."

Food wholesalers still plied their trade along Duane Street from their old brick buildings; trucks idled beneath overhanging metal awnings as teamsters loaded them with milk and cheese. The din was conveniently loud.

"I don't hear anything," he said.

"Let's get out of here." A dark triangle of park lay between Duane Street's legs. Within the small plot were dozens of sleepers wrapped in the blankets upon which, the next morning, they'd peddle magazines retrieved from dentist's offices. Bernard said it was easier, now, to live in Calcutta; it was never cold in Calcutta. Growing used to the pounding of the trucks' heartbeats I heard again what I didn't want to hear, footsteps racing with quicker rhythm than ours. Wishing I'd worn lower heels, I trotted leftward, Lester close behind. I heard the pop of a firecracker; having heard the sound, knew I hadn't yet been shot.

"God," I said. "Run!" We dashed up a side street on the north border of the square, our feet slipping over Belgian block. The street was so narrow that its low buildings seemed three times as high as they were; only a solitary lamppost broke the two-block gloom. An enclosed bridge of almost Venetian appearance ran between buildings nearest the light, several stories above the street. We could have as easily run into the last century and not known, so unalterably ancient were our surroundings. Where the dark was deepest we pressed ourselves into a wall.

"Why are we running?" Lester asked as we waited.

"They're shooting."

"Who?" I shook my head, imagining a deli's wealth of selections. The assailants of Jensen, working their way through the repertoire; Jake, having acted upon second thoughts; soldiers taking target practice, a sniper warming up before performance, an accountant upset with her husband. Some shot only for the love of the sound.

"Anybody after you besides us?" I asked.

"Not anymore," he said. "Do you think he's behind it?"

"We'd never know. Gus would be handling it if that's the case—"

"The old guy?"

"He's had experience—"

"Breaking children's fingers?"

"He shot three Presidents." All remained quiet, but it didn't matter. Patience was all; we couldn't move, if we were to be missed. Had I been left to simmer in my own juices I might never have moved again. A door slammed, down where the trucks waited to pull out, and I glanced at their lights. When I turned around I saw Lester walking into the middle of the dead street to wait there, as if to see who might notice. As he stood beneath the streetlamp's half-light, Lester almost appeared to glow from within, his aura assuredly no less radioactive than numinous.

"Nothing's happened to us yet, Joanna," he said. Returning to where I stood, fastened onto the brick, he took my arm and pulled me away. Down on Duane Street the trucks revved, pulling out to make their deliveries. My stomach burned as if my ulcers were newly aflame; I sank to my knees, my strings cut. Wanting to throw up, I threw out only near-tears, crying without wet, without sound, that no others might see, or hear, and so gain awareness I didn't want them to have. "No," he said. "It's all right. It is." As he stroked my back I began to recover, drawing long, dry breaths; my head reattached itself to my body. "A truck backfiring. Must have been. If somebody was after us we've given them plenty of opportunity."

"They have that anyway," I said; it did seem safe enough, for the moment. Lester helped me to my feet; when we walked off I noticed the street's name. I'd never heard of Staple Street but others must have, for they lived there. A nearby window showed kitchenlight; boxes of catfood on the sill, a dead plant, a plastic hanukiah. We turned right, toward Hudson Street.

"This happen to you often?" Lester asked. My mouth ached as I answered, so harshly had I bridled myself against my tears.

"It didn't used to," I said. "This is too much. I hate being afraid all the time. I hate what I am. How I live—"

"Don't say that."

"I hate what I've done. What they've done to me. I hate so much and I can't let it out." So often so-called new men purport to admire the inherent gentleness of women, only demonstrating they know women no better than old men; too often a woman recirculates her rage through herself, settling upon the likeliest victim in the most practical way. Men play at anger, as at a game; so many times, in those days, I too could have taken a machete and hacked through any subway-car's passengers, but for a reason.

"You hate what you've let them do to you?" he asked.

"That too." Hudson Street looked so much more of our time than had Staple Street that you could almost imagine people still using it. Cars two to twenty years old lined the curbs. Traffic restrictions ended a block below Canal Street, and as we drew closer the streets began filling with traffic. On the city entrance of the Holland Tunnel, at the end of Canal, the Army ran a haphazard checkpoint, stopping and searching vehicles for improprieties that might be seized and resold. The line of cars awaiting entrance into the city ran, at all hours, five miles deep into Jersey; Dryco and Army cars had their own lane, and so passed more easily. The rumor was that the soldiers, to cut costs, reused their testing needles on their successive suspects.

"We cross north?" Lester asked. No taxis grazed our flanks as we raced across Canal; no tanks flattened us, rolling down their center lane. One of several double-length semis almost blew us over with its wind, careening past. On the trailer was the Kraft logo; superimposed upon that, the Dryco smile.

"You were right, what you said. I'd trust a stranger before I'll trust a friend."

"For the right reasons?" Lester asked.

"Friends always expect you to behave in a certain way. When you don't, sometimes, they're disappointed, some-times they hate you. Sometimes I think people have friends only to make sure they can always be hurt."

"So you behave differently around strangers," he said.

"I'm looser," I said. "Thatcher likes everyone high-strung. And the people I've known the longest and have been the closest to are also the biggest liars I know, so—"

"How much do you think has rubbed off on you?"

On the far corner an enormous office building had been torn down years before for luxury apartments never built. Hundreds of smaller residences were scattered across the lot in its stead: boxes and crates, ill-pitched tents, tin-walled huts, clusters of cardboard. At the neighborhood's center stood a small frame shack, surely the home of that commu-nity's Thatcher.

"Enough, I'm afraid," I said. "I used to have so many more friends."

"What happened to them?"

"Bankrupt between breakfast and lunch," I said. "Lost their jobs. Their apartments. If I saw them I wouldn't know them now."

"You would," said Lester.

"It was just luck it didn't happen to me," I said. "Bernard moved to Dryco just before. I moved as well. The right place, the right time. I couldn't help it."

"It's all right—"

"It'd never happen again," I said. "Everything hinges on his behavior. My life depends on how crazy he gets. I don't like it."

Along these blocks the remnant of a more traditional neighborhood remained: a diner, a deli, a row of shops partially rented. In the deli window was a sign written in Korean and English, reading *Japs Keep Out*, looking so old as to refer to Axis-allied Japan. The doors of stores were open to catch cool evening breezes. Two young girls thrashed about on the sidewalk, arguing and cursing, pinning one another with pipestem legs; they looked Jake's age, or younger. A gang of boys hooted; several older men watched, keeping their hands in their pockets. The girls screamed, oblivious to sideshow eyes.

"You said that older man killed three Presidents," Lester said. Three teenagers, their shaved heads making them resemble mad insects, shoved by us as they made for the brawl. "Who was the third?"

"Gus was on the grassy knoll," I said. The crowd's scream faded to a whisper, the farther we drew from it. Lester took so long to respond that I wondered if he'd heard me.

"You're serious?"

"That's what Thatcher told me. As I understand it Gus didn't know Oswald was there until they started shooting. I suppose they were as shocked as anyone."

"Who fired the shot that killed him?"

"Gus isn't sure," I said.

One last small shop sold mineral specimens, petals of stone, roses plucked from the rock. I doubted the doctors had a lease. After that the street passed through dead blocks, every building's windows and storefronts boarded up as against the flood. Flowered decals brightened some windows' blinders. Sprigs of colorless grass sprouted through the broken sidewalk. So abandoned in haste did all appear that I imagined entering any of the buildings, finding coffee still warm in cups, toothpaste still wet upon brushes, and not even a scrap to show where everyone went.

"That your company's mark?" Lester asked, pointing toward an upper floor. Plastered below the cornices were block-long posters advertising the new development shortly rising on that lot. They'd missed the target completion date by three years. It seemed too late to idly seek logos, but at last I saw what he saw, a small design in no way resembling Dryco's empyrean leer.

"Bank of Nippon," I said. "Their mark. These are some more frozen assets. I'm sure he'll wind up with them eventually. I've lost track of half of what they have."

"Do they own everything?" Lester asked, seeming overly aware of what everything contained.

"Every business has a little bit of Dryco in it."

"How'd they do it?" he asked. "Luck? Did they plan it?"

"Their government reps found out about the revaluation before it went into effect," I said, explaining it as I'd heard it from Bernard. "Some of them suggested it. Before it went through the Drydens'd already traded the old money in for new bills. They wanted to see their competition in the drug field out of business as badly as the government did, of course. When the market crashed Susie was the only one able to buy. She bought fifty percent of seventy companies. That was all they needed."

"What was he doing at the time?"

"Conferring in Washington," I said. "By sunset the deals were done. I don't think either of them knew before it happened how far they'd be able to take it."

It was such an odd feeling to speak to another without interruption, certain too that I was being heard. "She seems the more pragmatic of the two," he said. "She knows about you and—"

I nodded. "Everybody knows, I think. Sometimes I talk to Avi about it. Bernard never wants to hear." Somewhere to the north something blew up. I wondered if we'd find my house where I'd left it. "Thatcher was sort of a rebound, after Avi."

On the side of a building was another aging billboard, this one older than many. *God Sees Those Who Come Unto Him* was the message printed below the photo. Swastikas were scrawled across the picture's faces, the survivors on their day of liberation. Avi's father had been in Maidanek during most of the war. With his family he left Crown Heights when the Army entered Brooklyn. Avi sent half of his salary every month to their upstate shtetl. Does he know how you earn your money? I asked him, on our last night.

He knows a purpose beyond understanding, Avi replied.

A guard's supposed to defend. Thatcher says kill and you go after anyone he wants.

It's my job.

Nazi, I called him.

There's no comparison. The Drydens are like a mother animal rolling over and suffocating her young as she sleeps.

They're not so unconscious.

Nor are you, he said, kissing my hands. I allowed myself to reenter my unavoidable world. "Joanna?" Lester asked. "You there?"

"I'd never thought about Thatcher before," I said. "Not in that way. Not until later. So much could have been avoided. I might still be myself."

"Maybe," said Lester. "They provide maps without roads. We have to hack our own path."

"They," I repeated. "Are there really two of Them?"

"Way I describe it isn't strictly accurate," he said. "Problem of popularizing. Everybody understands, at least, way I tell it. The split between Their aspects is a decided one, I'm never sure which One I'm hearing until I listen a spell. And I can always talk to Them, see, but They don't always talk to me."

"But you can talk to Them—"

"Not incessantly," he said, "and They don't tell me everything."

"If They're separate," I asked, "what tore Them apart?"

Signs noting curfew were so peppered by gunblasts that they could have been used as graters. As two halftracks rumbled downtown no fresh shots rang out, no footsteps echoed but our own, and none in command chose to stop us for interrogation. I dreamed of safety, so close to home. "Creation," he said.

"How?"

"A difficult birth," he said. "Whether They're truly split, I'd hate to say. I'm not sure that They even know. It's a spiritual division more than a physical, I believe."

"If They are split," I said, "could They ever reunite?"

He nodded. "There's a problem in that."

"What else is new?—"

"If They do, the world will be made anew. But that means the world as we know it must end."

"It must?" I asked. "You know that?"

"They pull up the corner of a blanket sometimes and show me what's underneath. When They feel like it They show me something else. It's up to me to draw the inferences. The blind men and the elephant, nothing more."

King Street was a block away; something hung from my corner's lamppost but it didn't look as if it had ever been alive. Tank-treads rutted the new-tarred pavement, looking as fossils on the land. "Thanks for walking with me," I said. "I live around the corner. Would you like to come in?"

"Sure."

"I'm sorry I ask so many questions," I said.

"You know the story of Job?" Hearing no response, he

65

continued. "Job questioned God. God questioned Job in return. They made an arrangement and Job returned to his life. Years later a stranger called on Job, demanding to know the answer to a question. 'He tells you to speak to Him as an equal and you let Him treat you like that?' the stranger asked, and Job answered, 'Listening to Him as He spoke I realized that the Creator may need neither sense nor sanity to do as He does, and that our failings in such may be more godlike than we know. It seemed most reasonable to agree with everything He said.'"

I brushed the day's debris from my steps with my foot into a neat pile at the bottom. My neighbor screamed, welcoming us home; Lester seemed afraid until he saw I could no longer respond to her voice. Bernard once told me how the screams of children in his building kept him awake at night. "That wasn't all that happened," Lester continued. "'You have no more questions?' God asked Job, he told the stranger, and Job had one more question, but worried that he'd tested God too much, and so for an endless time only mouthed the word with his lips. 'You don't learn if you don't ask,' God said.

"'Why?' Job finally asked, but God was gone."

FIVE

· · · ·

Switching off the alarms I flipped on the overheads, bringing light throughout my house. "This is all your place?" Lester asked, hovering behind me as if fearful to step further into the entry. Once he came in I reset the alarm, locked the five locks, slid the police bar back up. If anyone lay in wait I had a gun in my purse, but I had never had to use it.

"Plus the floor upstairs. They call it a duplex but it's enough for thirty. It's Thatcher's place, really. A gift until he wants it back."

The previous owners favored the sort of decor that resulted in its having appeared in expensive journals, years before. Most of the rooms were the width of the house, divided by walls painted in Navaho white and floored with blond wood. Lester wandered through the living room, narrowing his eyes against the glare of the furniture, and studied an abstract I had hanging above the fireplace. Looking anew into its painted swirls I wondered how my friend had known what angels swarmed over heaven.

"It's called 'Driven to Pieces in Pursuit of Love,'" I said. "A girlfriend of mine painted it. She did a number of works that no one ever bought. Except this one."

"It's awful dark," he said. "She did this recently?"

It was dark; the angels smothered in vast clouds of dust, tumbling wing over wing as they spiraled into the deep. "She bought a factory loft in Tribeca," I said. "Her fiancé came down to see the place. She stepped into the elevator to take him up to the roof to show him, but the elevator wasn't there."

"I'm sorry," Lester said.

"She'd be even unhappier now than she was then," I said. "You want a drink?"

"Bourbon'd be good," he said. "A little one."

"I wouldn't want to corrupt."

"Don't worry," he said. We entered my apartment's Food Preparation/Interpersonal Interaction Core; here the designers had so unyieldingly followed a black and white pattern in both fixture and wall that, entering the room, one felt to have fallen into a crossword puzzle. There were burners and microwaves and convection ovens; cabinets and blenders and gadgets enough to supply large restaurants. In a cabinet I kept one knife, one fork, one spoon, and two plates.

"I've never seen a refrigerator this large," he said, staring at its bulk; Bulganin refrigerators were the finest made, I'd heard, but I suppose Russians understood ice. It was large enough to hold half a steer. "Entertain much?"

I poured our drinks into the two glasses I kept ready for socializing. "Bernard tells me I more often depress." When I handed Lester his bourbon he took small sips, as if drinking too rapidly might sear shut his mouth. "Strong enough?"

"I don't drink much," he said, sitting on a black stool, leaning against a white countertop. "I don't see what got him so interested in me. It's not as if I just started doing this."

"I have no idea," I said. "I think he thinks he can use you to intimidate."

"Intimidate who?"

"A limitless number of candidates."

"Seems he sees too many squirrels in the trees," said Lester. "What does he think I am, anyway?"

"It should be obvious," I said. "It *was* obvious; he only wanted to hear me say it. "He thinks that if you're not the messiah, he can use you as such."

"To intimidate," Lester said, smiling, not appearing happy. He ran his fingertip around his glass's rim as if to make it sing.

"He's been playing it cagey. He's impossible to figure out after a point, he doesn't even tell his wife what he's up to—"

"Would it be more to my advantage to be the messiah or to pretend to be the messiah?"

"Same difference," I said. "He'll keep working on you."

"She seems preoccupied with something besides me," he said. "What else is going on that might tie in to his plans?"

"A member of our organization was murdered without our consent," I said. "He's already decided who's guilty, and you never know what the punishment'll be until—"

"Murdered?" Lester said.

"It's business," I said. "What do you expect?"

"That's why you were so afraid," he said. "When you thought somebody was shooting at us."

I nodded.

"Then he's meeting a Japanese representative on Tuesday. Bernard's cooked up some treaty of alignment. Thatcher isn't keen to go along. He tends to see connections where none exist, and I think he's seeing a connection between the murder and the alignment. The Drydens are dysfunctional unless they're lurching from crisis to crisis—"

"Then sometime I might wind up as part of a connection too?" Lester asked.

For several moments I stared into my drink's melting ice, gazing into smooth translucence as if to read the future; saw nothing that comforted or disturbed. "You might. I might. You never can tell."

"That must make for uncertainty . . ."

I nodded. "Once he gets his paws on you he'll adhoc it for awhile, until something gets rolling. Figure he'll set his sights low to start."

"It's good to have low expectations," said Lester. "Messianic hopes are the worst kind. He's bound to be disappointed."

"He doesn't like to be disappointed," I said. "Show him the angels. That'd shut him up."

"He couldn't see them," said Lester. "Not even if he wanted to. Are you sorry you saw them?"

"I'm not sorry," I said. "I'm not glad."

"They were glad to see you."

"Must be pretty boring up there, then," I said, standing and rinsing my glass in the sink; pondering for an instant if I should fix myself another one before picking up the bottle, and pouring again. "I'm sure Bernard'll be stuck with the details, if you were to go along. He always has to tie up the loose ends."

"What do people expect of a messiah?" Lester asked. "People in general, I mean. What do you think?"

"How should I know? It's nothing I've ever thought about," I said. "Somebody to clean up the mess, I suppose. Bring about a better world. Cure disease, rebuild cities, sweep the streets." My soul's Bernard eased out again before I felt it breaking the surface; I barely contained my laugh as I enumerated. "Wash the dishes, fix the sink, make the bed—"

"People can do those things," said Lester. "The big things and the small."

"But they won't. They don't even try anymore. Too afraid they'll fail, I suppose, and so they stop caring, or pretending to care—"

"As I understand it," said Lester, "They love us most when we try and fail."

"Lessens the competition," I said. "It'll never happen in any event, so there's no point discussing it." I marveled at how manipulative I could be; watched his face to see what reaction might appear there. It wasn't that I was drunk, for I wasn't; I only wanted to test him as he seemed to be forever testing me.

"The messiah will come," he said. "Not the one anybody wants or expects."

A memory rose up in my mind; I saw again the books in my parents' den, their books and the dusty volumes passed down from my mother's grandfather, shoved into the highest shelves, unread for years. One afternoon when I was thirteen I remembered climbing up and poking around, seeing what I might find there. He was a rabbi; most of his old books were in Hebrew and I could never read those. Some were in English, and I recalled coming across a paragraph concerning Waldo Frank as I idly flipped pages, the dust rising, steam from a lone riders' white donkey. Frank believed that when the messiah came the messiah would come as a woman; it occurred to me what an unfathomable, yet charming concept that seemed. The rest of the book was drier than the dust that covered it; I replaced it on the shelf, and ran outside to soak up sunlight and let the wind blow the dust from my skin.

"How do They feel about the messiah?" I asked. "Have They told you?"

"They know that when the messiah comes They'll re-unite, but They don't know what'll happen after that. They know that everything will change, but They don't know how, and so They've never been in any rush—"

"So They'll keep putting it off."

"It's almost time," he said. "They've had all Their doubts confirmed, at this point. It must give Them pause. You could say the messiah's Their doomsday device."

Picking up the CD's remote I switched on the radio, tuned as always to WNEW-AM; "Highway 61" rang out through the apartment's speakers, and I quickly switched it off.

"Want another drink?" I asked; he shook his head. "Want to see the rest of the place?"

As we walked through I showed him the backyard garden, the dining room, the two bathrooms on the first floor. Pictures of my parents hung on the stairway's wall, and he examined them.

"You favor your mother," he said. The shot he saw was taken on their twentieth anniversary, when she was a year younger than I was then.

"She colored her hair," I said. "She went gray early on."

"They live in town?"

I preserved what remained of them: odd pieces of small furniture, some books, my dishes; a family album, images trapped in black and white amber. My father stood in Penn Station's iron greenhouse with his fellow soldiers in those old photos; my mother skipped rope on Pitkin Avenue, in Brooklyn, in long-erased Brownsville. Sometimes I found photos of myself that I couldn't recall being taken, shots where my color was grayed by distance and time, and I looked no more than a child hired for an ephemeral event. For so long I remembered my dreams so much more clearly than I remembered my past.

"They're dead," I told him. "I grew up in Short Hills, in Jersey. They sold the house a few years after Dad retired."

He'd bought it for ten thousand, sold it for seven hundred thousand; were I to have repurchased it myself, that day, I would have paid the same number of dollars as he paid but the cost would have been so much greater. It was a comfortable house, near the arboretum and the train station; in those woods I knew my first boys. In the backyard was a gas grill, layered with the ash and soot of a thousand barbecues; I remembered staring into its flames as a child, thinking how cool those icy blue feathers looked.

"I guess they were old . . ."

"They were young," I said. "They moved to a retirement community. In Florida. After the revaluation they lost their savings. They couldn't afford the maintenance on their co-op and they got an eviction notice. I didn't know until later. They must not have wanted me to worry, and I never thought—"

"Joanna, it's all right . . ."

"Let's go upstairs," I said. He preceded me on the ascent. The second floor's vacuums were broken, and dust settled over us as might sea-mist at the shore. "They didn't tell me. It was such a—"

"Joanna?"

"Such a—" I began again, unable to think of a suitable conclusion.

"Are you all right?"

"Fine," I said. "I'm fine. They were fine. Their lives went so smoothly. Too smoothly. I'd learned not to worry about them."

"Joanna, it wasn't your fault, whatever happened—"

"I should have been there," I said, stopping, leaning against the wall; I'd not let myself think about it since it happened. They'd decided upon their course of action with the logic they brought to all situations; decided to kill themselves, and so obtained poison from a reliable source. "Why didn't they tell me?"

"Joanna, it's all right," he said, holding me as if to keep

73

me from shaking. Every Saturday night they fixed a candle-light dinner for themselves, once I was old enough that I might make my own arrangements. I remembered so often leaving the house, seeing them sitting there, staring into each other's eyes as if they'd been married the day before. Perhaps, that night, they'd hoped to draw such romance as they could from their final tableau; more likely the electricity had been cut off, and they needed candlelight in order to measure out their doses. A candle caught the bedroom drapes on fire, the fire department said; they'd passed out before blowing out the lights.

"I didn't know," I said. Mom could have slept through it; Dad got halfway across the living room. "The fire department sent me a bill for their services the next day on the fax. That's how I found out—"

"It's all right," Lester repeated, not letting me go. "It's all right. Go ahead and cry—"

"I can't," I said. "I haven't been able to in years. Not really."

They wanted their ashes sprinkled over Coney Island, where they'd met. Early one morning, the next week, Avi drove me out to the beach and stood guard to make sure no one else came near. I walked out to the surf; almost jabbed my foot on a needle. The wind was blowing; I tried to wait until it settled, but a gust came along as I let go of the ashes and they blew back onto the beach, mixing with the gray sand until I couldn't tell where they'd gone.

"You're crying now," he said; they ran down my cheeks.

"No—"

"You are—"

"Not really," I said. "Come on," I said, pulling away from him, wiping my face dry. "I'm sorry. Let's go on. Up here."

At the top of the stairs we turned, and walked down a short hall. "This is my bedroom," I said as we walked in, seeing my bed, my dresser and the television as I'd left them. When I turned on the lights I turned on the set as well, hoping that something distracting might be playing. A commercial was on; to sell watches the narrator quoted the second law of thermodynamics as an old Otis Redding song drifted over the images of women nearly nude and dyed blue. I couldn't deal with such neopost so late, and turned it off.

"Better?" he asked. I nodded. "You have a beautiful home."

"Thatcher has a beautiful home," I said. "I didn't mean to get so upset. It's just—"

"I shouldn't have brought it up," he said, touching my face. "Don't worry. Everything's all right."

"I haven't been able to cry for so long," I said, sitting on the bed. "I was all dried up. It hurt too much to feel so much. I couldn't. I'm sorry—"

"You can cry around me," he said. "Joanna, there's nothing wrong in that—"

"I haven't cried since that last night with Avi," I said. "Not since then. Thatcher'll never see me cry."

Lester sat down next to me, keeping distance enough that while I could take comfort from his nearness I wasn't pressed into some unwarranted embrace. As I tried to calm myself I took deep breaths, drawing as much air into my lungs as I could; feeling, as Jake surely had, that I had killed without reason. "You and Avi must have been very close," he said.

"It's funny," I said, "we broke it off just as we were getting closest. That's how it always seems to work when you get to know someone too well, I think. Peel off one too many layers of skin and then you can't bear the touch any longer." I stood, straightening my skirt, and walked across the room to my closet where, ducking behind the door, I could peer into the mirror there to see what a shambles I had made of my face. With tissue and cream I removed my makeup, kicking off my shoes as I stood there, out of Lester's sight. "So where do you live?"

"Around," he said. "It's good to keep moving."

"You're originally from Tennessee?"

"Kentucky," he corrected. "Everybody up here always confuses them. I grew up near Lexington. My mother's folks came from over the mountain."

"What's it like down there?" Some of Thatcher's friends owned horse farms in the state, and at every business function were prone to weave shimmering tales of the plantation life. I'd always suspected they'd poured us watered bourbon. "It always looks so pretty in the pictures."

"I haven't been there in years," he said. "I don't know what's left. It's probably like everywhere else by now."

"When I moved out," I said, unbuttoning my blouse, "I didn't go home again for months. I understand how it is." When he said nothing in reply I wondered if I possibly could understand. "Why do they call it the Bluegrass?"

"Don't know. It's the same grass as in Central Park, I think. Just as brown."

I shut the closet door, coming into his sight once more wearing only my slip and undergarments. Could a messiah desire, I wondered; I didn't see why not. He didn't look away as he saw me, but neither did he seem pleased; his cheeks flushed red, as if he'd received a sudden transfusion. "Are your parents still down there?"

"Yes," he said. "They built a Toyota plant across the road from where our house was, I heard. It must be closed if it hasn't gone out of business, I suppose. Probably Dryco will reopen it one day—"

"Probably," I said, walking toward him.

"Do you want me to leave the room while you change clothes?"

"No." So often during my life I knew a suspicion, that for periods of time not all of my actions were my own; that a loved one's dybbuk rose from the void to settle for awhile in my body, and know the life inside my head. Reaching down, I began unbuttoning his shirt, staring at my hands, seeing another's. He remained so still that I might have been undressing a mannequin.

"You're very pretty, Joanna," he said.

"You don't think I'm fat?" Thatcher once told me he could set a teatray on my ass and I'd never notice until I sat down, and he intended it as a compliment. "I don't take very good care of myself."

"It wouldn't matter—" he said. He showed a certain reluctance as I pulled his shirt from his body, but made no move to stop me. In clothes he seemed slim; now I saw how wiry he was, how tightly his muscles were drawn across his bones. Then, seeing his right side, I backed quickly away, feeling as he must have felt in the hall, when he asked about my parents. From his waist to his armpit his skin appeared as strip-mined as any Kentucky mountainside, pitted where it should have been smooth, smooth where it should have been rippled. The original design was forever lost.

"Who shot you?" I asked; Avi had similar scars. For the first time since we'd met he averted his own eyes.

"It was deer season," he said, laughing. "Hunter mistook me for a cow." So many men lie as if to their mothers, stammering out denials with such bravado and so blatantly that one could only imagine that they dreamed of being caught.

"Lester—"

"It was a while back," he said. "Didn't hit anything important. The newspapers called me the miracle child."

"What happened?"

He shook his head; for the moment I let the subject drop. "You're lucky you lived," I said; he seemed uncertain how he might respond, and so said nothing. He wore the semblance of a smile on his lips, as if, having heard an old family joke for the umpteenth time, he had done his duty by responding as if he'd heard it all anew. I sat in my dresser's chair, facing him.

"We can't, Joanna," he said. "I wouldn't feel right."

It should have been understandable, and was, and I was sorry all the same. He shrugged, and folded up his shirt. "It's all right . . ." I said.

"Their means are difficult, whatever Their ends," he said. How long, I wondered, had he told himself there was a purpose before he finally believed it? Against his better judgment had he wound up hoping, after all, instead of knowing? As I looked at him I watched him shiver, as if the room was as cold as Thatcher's. Maybe somebody walked over his grave.

"Do you ever think about Kentucky?" I asked.

"I'm not much for nostalgia." We sat there a few minutes more, wordless and slumped, at last eroding beneath our rain of events, this heaven-sent plague.

"Will you stay here tonight anyway?" I asked. "To talk?"

"I'll stay longer," he said. "You have questions?"

"They must have given you some answers," I said.

"Not the sort of answers anyone wants to hear. What questions do you mean?"

"Is there an afterlife?" I asked.

"What's the matter with the one you have?"

"Say there is," I said. "Say there was a more perfect world beyond ours. Why would They keep this one, in that case?"

"Why do you think?" he asked in return. I lay down; Lester remained seated.

"Practice," I said. "They couldn't bear to part with the original. They kept it as an object lesson."

He nodded, and looked away from me, pondering his own questions. "I can't help but disappoint him," he said. "When that happens, what'll he do to me?"

"Depends on how disappointed he is," I said. "He's such a bastard. He'll hound me until I leave and hound you until you start, and it won't matter what happens in the process."

"He'd be right in that," said Lester. "Perhaps it'll lessen

the damage to go ahead and get things underway with him, then—"

I shook my head. "Disappear before he has a chance to get you. It's not worth getting involved. You don't know what you'll do until he makes you do it, and then it's too late. Don't give him the chance."

"It's a chance that must be followed through on," he said. "There's a purpose for what has to be done. I can't go anywhere, Joanna. I have to do as I'm told. I doubt I'll need to be at the company very long."

"Then I won't leave until you do."

"I know," he said. "Such a strange organization. The immediate circle he seems to rule over as if it were a family."

"He does," I said. "He and Susie take turns doing the beating while the other looks on. They're no more dysfunctional than most, they're simply more adept at it."

"Families have misunderstandings," he said. "After a while they stop seeing one another. Each member becomes no different from anyone else passed on the street." He stood; I stared at the ceiling as intently as I could, attempting to conjure up angels of my own.

"Everyone goes blind after so long," I said. "That night Avi and I talked, he said anyone could become a Nazi once they stopped seeing their Jews."

"Was it his child you had?" Lester asked. I couldn't see his face from where I lay. He stood near my dresser, and I knew he was examining the pair of booties I had hanging on the knob of the mirror's frame. "These weren't yours, were they? You'd have had them bronzed—"

"I knitted them," I said.

"You had a baby?"

"Once."

"Recently?" he asked, walking over and sitting next to me, gazing down as if he might peer directly into my mind.

"January," I said. "Things happen." As I shut my eyes he leaned closer, whispering:

"Where's your baby?"

"Where're your parents?"

The effect was as desired; he said nothing else. After a second or so he walked over and switched off the room's light, returning to my bed and lying beside me, facing away. As we bundled in silence my eyes accepted the dark, and I saw in his silhouette his side's unnatural curve. Keeping my touch as light as a butterfly's, I landed fingertips onto his back, feeling hard rubber sheathed in satin, a tuft of lamb's wool at the root of his spine. When I began to cry again I pulled away from him. He clasped me as I rolled over. I remembered my father holding me as a child, and I, feeling so safe; I had never wanted to feel safe again, never before asked for protection—never believed I deserved it when so many others lived and died without imagining there could be such a thing.

"I'm sorry, Joanna," he said. "It's difficult to tell what you want to talk about."

"Feeling's mutual," I said, feeling my face become warmer and wetter. "You make me remember too much. I feel like I'm on overload, my head can't hold it all—"

"It's impossible to remember too much," he said. "Everything should be remembered. So much is lost over time. Every moment should be honored for having existed, even the bad ones."

"Every moment," I repeated, knowing I could never recall a thousandth of my own. "Why would They send a messiah if They don't even know what'll happen? Why would They risk it?"

"They have hopes," he said, placing his head on the pillow next to mine, looking, in the dark, so tired.

"You said you could predict our futures," I said. "What are they?"

"Unavoidable," he said, putting his arm across my shoulder. As he touched me I felt the fine hair rise from the nape of my neck. Why do the heathern rage? Why not? A siren outside sang through the night, the scream of an onrushing train. "You know why everyone has this?" he asked, tapping the shallow groove between my nose and upper lip.

"I don't even know what it's called."

"Before you were born you knew all there is," he told me. "You knew the beginning and the end. You knew why the dinosaurs died, why blue is blue. You knew why pain doesn't ennoble us and why we wouldn't be human without it. You knew what your life would hold." I touched my face, brushing his finger with my own. "When it was time for you to be born They pressed shut your lips, using an angel's thumb to make the print. The angels cried for having done it but knew it had to be done, you had to forget all you knew upon entering this world, because the one thing you'd have never known is how it feels, remembering it again."

Though we could never be lovers, as I kissed him I knew that feeling lovers know in their first minutes together, a false commingling of fear and relief and the peace that comes upon believing again that the world can be wonderful even in its illness. Our kiss, unlike an angel's thumb, did not press our memories away. At nine Monday morning we reported to work.

SIX

...

On Monday afternoon we discussed our newest project. "Don't try to deny you didn't have your doubts," said Thatcher. "I'd hate to think you were just humoring me."

"After Friday afternoon I never suspected anything would actually come of this," said Bernard. "I thought he'd race back to his flock and that'd be the last we heard of him."

"Told you I made arrangements." Susie looked at her husband; shook her head as if he'd told her he'd accidentally mowed down her flower beds.

"That shouldn't have changed things. By all rights he should've sprung up like a toadstool somewhere else. But perhaps hearing our words issuing from a different mouth decided the vote." Bernard turned to me, smiling with lips so perfectly curved, so remarkably still, that they might have been painted on his face.

"She's learning," said Thatcher.

"So if all's roses, what's the problem?" Susie asked, taking no shelter from the world behind sunglasses or newspaper this morning. Not even the residue of a smile showed on her face.

"The problem is that from here out I'll be working from theory alone," said Bernard. "As I understand it, you want to spread Macaffrey's cult of personality more thickly upon the populace."

"Without any public connection to us, just yet," said Thatcher. "We'll backchannel him, meantime, when we need him for company work."

"But what's desired? You want the audience entertained with sermons, blessings, the occasional odd miracle? You want to see what ripples result from tossing him in the pond?"

"Sounds good to start," said Thatcher. "You're acting like this is all something new to you, Bernard. You've just got to figure out the best way to sell a new product—"

"Apples and oranges," said Bernard. The gray world curtained the room's great window; it rained, several hundred feet beneath us.

"I don't get you—"

"How do you sell a messiah, Thatcher?" Bernard asked.

"Above cost," said Thatcher, laughing. "In the fastest way."

"You'd use television to do that?"

"How else?" Susie asked. "Weren't you referring to some tests last week you could run?"

"Tests, eventually. That's not the problem here. If the audience first sees Macaffrey on television, they won't see him."

"Don't give me analysis bullshit, Bernard, that doesn't make sense," said Thatcher. "What are you trying to say?"

"Explicate and deconstruct," Susie added.

Bernard rested his chin in his hand as if the weight of his

head had proved too great for his neck. "A car needs gas," he said. "A messiah needs belief. Nobody believes anything they see on television unless they've convinced themselves they could see it in real life. His followers would tune in every night, all twenty or thirty of them. Anyone else'll zap right past."

"We can put any damn foolishness we want to on TV and people believe it—"

"Apples and oranges," Bernard repeated. "When we put most things on television it's not to make them believe, it's to make what they're seeing their background. Assimilation is what you aim for with television. Shooting your image through the skull repeatedly that, eventually, enough of it sticks that it seems to have always been there. That won't work in the same way, this time."

"Eye the tube any day of the week," said Susie. "New faces show every hour. Hundreds megatime it once they get their minute, why shouldn't he if that's what's wanted?" Looking to her husband, she lowered her voice, speaking to him as if they sat beneath moonlight. "If he's a wash, cut losses all the sooner."

Bernard gnawed the end of his thumb, drawing from the cuticle a red droplet resembling a ladybug at rest. "Let's talk image equivalency," he said. "People appear on television. For a while someone might tune in specifically to see them. Then a fresh distraction appears on a different channel. Nobody knows what keeps people watching particular things. A democracy of images is impossible to deliberately subvert."

"We need the right sales pitch, Bernard—" said Thatcher.

"You're not pushing detergent. You want this fool to show up one night after the news, claiming to be God. You might as well put him on Telepsychic—"

"Negativity's showing," said Susie.

"Realism's showing. This necessitates serious real-world preparation, and even then, every time he appears on television a certain symbolic worth will be lost unless we exercise complete control over surrounding programming."

"Hell, we could do that," said Thatcher. "What if he got on and performed some miracle?"

Bernard shook his head, glancing at me holding back his laughter. "The only miracle Macaffrey seems able to perform is convincing otherwise sensible people that he's anything other than a sociopath. So what if he could work miracles? He could make the moon dance in the sky and no one would believe it unless they saw it for themselves. No one would. You know why? They'd be inside, watching it on television."

"Can anything be done?" Susie asked. "I say dispose."

"If you want this done right it'll be a longterm project," said Bernard. "Longterm projects take a long time. Face it."

"So how do you propose we do this?" Thatcher asked.

"News of this ilk is most effectively transmitted only by word of mouth," said Bernard. "The old-fashioned way. Not to say we can't push buttons later on. Stooges can be hired and trained to pass the disinformation we want passed, as you know. Computer networks can be used after the introductory period. We can't televise before attaining saturation. Once we can rest assured that he's finally seeable, he'll be heard as well." Bernard stood up to stretch, having freed himself of confining ideas. "I hate to admit it, but the timing is perfect for this tomfoolery. Our premillennial fields possess fertile ground."

"What's the timeline?" asked Susie.

"Two years, at least," said Bernard. "Unless interest flags before then."

For over two years Thatcher had lived with the awareness that when he wanted, he received. "Two years," he repeated. "It can't take that long—"

"It will," said Bernard. "Of course, we haven't fully examined the premise that Macaffrey has, in the first place, anything to say."

"We'll burn that bridge when we come to it," said Thatcher. "Where is he right now?"

"Gus is babysitting him in my office. I left the television on to keep them calm. They seemed to hit it off, which I find inconceivable. Dealing with Macaffrey's like dealing with an idiot savant, but then I suppose Gus has had so much practice with Jake—"

"I say disinvest," said Susie.

"That's what you've said all along, darlin'—" Thatcher began.

"Keelhaul," she said. "Let the sharks have him."

"Got to do some R and D first," said Thatcher. "I'm optimistic. He'll probably come in handy meanwhile. I got a few things in mind. Go to it, Bernard. I trust you." Susie seemed considerably more troubled by Thatcher's verbal cuddling of Bernard than she ever did of her husband's physical assaults upon me; her jealousy was always professional, and I doubted that she took me seriously enough to worry. Rarely was I jealous of Susie; then, essentially, because he admitted to hearing her when she spoke.

"Let's go see how our boy's doing, Joanna." Bernard rose to follow.

Thatcher motioned for him to retake his seat. "Fill Susie in on what we were talking about while we're gone," he said.

"There's something needs doing you're avoiding?" she asked. "Afraid you'll get your hands messy?"

"Darlin', there's such a thing as being too cynical. Come on down to your office when you're finished, Bernard. Call first."

Bernard's quarters were at the far end of our floor. Creeping through a lacing of halls, attempting to keep up with Thatcher, I let my eyes pass over the hundreds of photos attached to the walls, each holding the image of a Dryco product. I wondered to myself if the shot of Lester might be larger, for ideology's sake if for no other. When we spoke our sound bled into the building's breath, droning all around us as we wandered its lungs.

"You have a cat's smile," I said, seeing his grin swell so that I believed his face might burst. "Where's the canary?"

"Trying to swallow the cat, seems to me," he said. "We'll get into it momentarily, hon. Macaffrey can help us out a lot sooner than they think, that's for sure—"

"How?" I asked, almost running to keep up with his long stride.

"Ears," he said, shaking his head, glancing at the walls. "Can't tell you how pleased I am you and Macaffrey get along so well."

"That's big of you," I said. "I get along with anyone I can talk with."

"Talk? Looked like Siamese twins when you two came in this morning. Messiahs have a great need for affection, I guess."

"Thatcher, he's—"

"You must feel like a dinosaur," he added, with unsurprising tact. "Nothing wrong with robbing the cradle long as you're not the one has to change the diapers."

Unexpected chords transposed the melody of his song. Curious to discover how he might deal with the situation as he seemed to perceive it, I refrained from explaining the nature of my relationship with Lester, not that he had any right to know of it in the first place.

"I'm glad you're taking this so well," I said. "I thought you might be upset."

"Oh, hon, it's only business. We all play the whore sometime." Before I could comment on that remark he added: "How'd Bernard convince you to do it?"

"Bernard has nothing to do with this," I said. "I told you Lester came back here—"

"Oh," he said, looked at me, and smiled. "So it was your idea after all. That's a good sign. I knew my influence'd wear off on you eventually. That's real good."

You get nowhere participating in a conversation with a ventriloquist who perceives you only as a new dummy; I said nothing more. Lester and Gus stood beside the desk in Bernard's office, their backs turned toward the door. Gus circled around before we entered. The commercial playing on TV was one of Dryco's; the spot commanded the viewer to enjoy life. One inspiration after another onscreened as the narrator sang: pink children romped with golden dogs, Christmas lights of a dozen colors outlined the gables of a Victorian house, oreads and naiads lounged on skislope and surfside, barely hidden beneath particolored shreds of quilt; innumerable scenes of a perfect world's perfect people flashed by, scenes that to my eye could have been filmed perhaps on Mars, but never on Earth, not any longer.

"Who knows?" Thatcher asked.

"None but God." By this ritual Gus signaled that he'd deafened the room's ears and blinded its eyes. The windowpanes rattled as they vibrated within their frames, shaken by the air conditioner's wind, assuring that none without could eavesdrop by discerning the tones with which our voices caused the glass to waver. Thatcher, collapsing into the leather chair, lifted his feet onto the desk, knocking the photo of Bernard's wife against the drawing of their son. I sat next to Lester, on the sofa, took his hand and squeezed it.

"What have they done to you?" I asked.

"Bored me to death," he said. "Till we came in here, anyway. Gus and I get along pretty good."

"How's it hanging, Macaffrey?" asked Thatcher. "You need anything, just ask Joanna. She'll see to your every need. I guess you figured that out already—"

"Call me Lester."

"Nothing like a first-name basis. Lester, I got something I want you to take a look at. See if you can pick up anything from it."

"What do you want picked?"

"Anything in bloom," said Thatcher. "Here you go, bud. Looks like a list, doesn't it?" Lester studied the note for a minute after Thatcher passed it over to him. "Can you see who wrote it?"

"Of course not," said Lester. "Does this have anything to do with the employee who was murdered?"

I knew no more showed in my face than I noticed showing in Gus's; Thatcher tried to give the impression of one lobotomized, but his eyes held the most disconcerting blend of desire and fear, the look of a molester listening for unexpected interruptions, and finding himself knifed by his victim. He looked to me, as if wishing to see my confession; he saw nothing. "It does," he said. "Somebody's in something bad and I'd like to help 'em out before they get in over their head."

Lester, returning the note to Thatcher, wriggled himself deeper into the sofa, that his shoulders might brush against mine. "I'm sure you have the best intentions. What do you know about the note so far?"

"Mahaica's name of a port in Guyana," said Thatcher. "Michael Moseley is the pseudonym of a local exporter down there, we're pretty sure—"

"Mystic means the one in Connecticut," Lester said.

Thatcher received this knowledge as if hearing the weather report, and I could only imagine that the earlier shock was still insulating his system from the effects of repeated jolts. "You're sure about that?" Lester nodded. "How?"

"I don't know why," said Lester. "It came to me."

Thatcher looked Lester over as if measuring him for size. "That's to be expected, I suppose. All right, then. Sounds likely as anything. Let's take it and fly. Hey, Gus? Seem to you there might be something to interest us in Mystic?"

"It could seem that way."

"Look into it. It's funny, you know," he said, taking two folded documents from his jacket pocket. "You never know what'll turn up where. Looked for one thing this weekend and found something else entirely. Something might shine a different light on Jensen's killing, seems to me."

"What?"

"He's not dead."

Early on in our relationship Thatcher conceived the notion that his secretary was attempting to eavesdrop upon his office conversations by means of radio waves, projected through the fillings in his teeth. After she was retired, electronic equipment was found in her desk; it was never discovered for whom she also worked. Though Thatcher's manias were many—and in my absence he could have fallen prey to any of them—there could be no discounting the possibility he might, again, be right.

"I know a dead man when *I* see one," said Gus.

"You never saw him dead," Thatcher said. "Close to death, but that's not close enough."

"Where is he, then, if he's still alive?"

"Don't you think I'm trying to find out? Now, if there'd been a body, would it have gone to Campbell's in accordance with the usual perks?"

Gus nodded. "Personnel would have handled arrangement, not Security."

"I am correct, though?"

"As an unmarried employee," Gus answered, "Jensen's body would have been taken to Campbell's for standard treatments and the cremains would have been urned as per."

"We'd never have known he didn't make it to Campbell's if I hadn't called to follow up. Funeral records aren't automatically sent to our floor, it seems. Things get too damn compartmentalized in this outfit. From here on out, anybody in this company sneezes, I want their file on my desk. Got me?"

"Because the body didn't get there doesn't mean he's still alive—"

"You think somebody wanted a souvenir?"

"What did the doctors say?" I asked.

"Depends on which one you talk to. The ones seeming most culpable are presently being talked to." Thatcher paused. "They're still kicking. We'll see."

"When were they brought in?"

"Last night," said Thatcher. "They're denying they know anything, but if so, they're just as guilty. We might have to bring their families into this. Might help 'em remember, showing 'em that carrot on the stick."

"Why wasn't I told?" Gus asked, sounding no less angry than Thatcher. "As Head of Security, why wasn't I told?" Lester said nothing through all of this, watching intently as if struck dumb by the workings of industry made flesh.

"Be realistic, Gus," said Thatcher. "You were up on the estate with us. You think I wanted to send you down to New York and leave us unprotected?"

"By a force of sixty-five—"

"Avi took care of the situation. And I did have to be sure you and Jake weren't in on this in any way. I've ascertained matters to my satisfaction now."

"You didn't trust us?" Gus asked, his face darkening. "You didn't trust me?"

"If I didn't trust you, Gus, would I be telling you now?"

Something seemed to have shifted within Thatcher's personality, on one hand allowing him to speak so freely about company business with comparative strangers present; on the other showing every sign of having locked that personality behind yet another door.

"What were you looking for that you found this out?" I asked, hoping to distract them before anything could go further. "What did you find out, besides what you say?"

"On Sunday," Thatcher said, "I asked Beekman to send up a copy of the attending physician's report," he said, passing a Xerox across. "I wanted to see the medical word.

Tests they got now, they can tell what bay the fish they took the poison from came out of. Anyway." He leaned forward; the chair groaned beneath his weight. "The average person wouldn't notice a thing wrong with those, don't you think?"

"Whose thumb?" Lester asked; Thatcher smiled. A seeming shadow showed at second glance to be a long thumb lying atop the line where the attending physician was to sign.

"Be nice to think whoever did this did it intentionally," said Thatcher, "but I'd be fooling myself. Sort of gives one pause, doesn't it? If the rest of the gang's no smarter than this, running 'em down'll be easier than pissing on ants."

"Whose signature is hidden?" I asked.

"I wondered that myself," said Thatcher. "So I had Avi go down and bring back the original by hand. He called ahead, they told him they'd looked but couldn't find it. When he went there he took Jake along. They found it."

"Jake went with him?" Gus asked. "He said nothing to me—"

"Well, I asked him not to, Gus. You understand." Thatcher passed me the original. "Shame they don't teach penmanship like they used to."

"This doctor," Gus said, his mouth tight, "is in custody?"

"No—" When Thatcher wanted to laugh but desired more strongly to keep a straight face his feet would shake, his joy finding its outlet by passing directly into the ground. His shoes tapped against Bernard's family photos, knocking them over. "I remembered the front page of the *News*, morning after Jensen's little melodrama. It was the sort of thing sticks with me." I remembered Susie's paper that day; remembered a photo beneath the headline CRUSH HOUR. A woman walking to work was pinned between a tank and parked cars, trying to cross the street. The photographer took his shot as the tank rolled away. "Probably wouldn't have made the front page if she hadn't been a doctor."

"Her signature?"

Thatcher smiled. "They probably had it ready before he was even brought in. Doubt she knew about it. Sure as hell bet they had it ready before they brought *her* in. If they even realized it, they probably just hoped nobody'd notice. She and Jensen must have been in ER at the same time, but I doubt they had much to say to each other. Which doctor you say you'd spoken to?"

"One of the residents," Gus said. "Doctor Lao. Young Chinese woman. Our doctors took over the case from her when they arrived."

"When the bastards washed the ink off their hands, you mean. Took over the case and when enough time passed, they told you he died. She backs you up, all right—"

"I don't need backup—"

"We talked awhile," Thatcher said. "I hired her, by the way. I'd started to think they might even have made up the cause of near-death, but she'd seen fugu poisoning before, when she was an intern. Some toxiterrorist used it in San Francisco while she was out there. When she heard Jensen hadn't pulled out of it she said she was shocked. Told me she never dreamed he wouldn't."

"Why?"

"Didn't have a strong enough dose, she didn't think," Thatcher said. "Strong enough to cause problems, sure. See, when you go into storage like that not enough blood tends to reach the brain. She said he'd probably been under long enough he wouldn't ever be *all* right again. Now whoever did it, for whatever reason, you know what I think they wound up doing?"

We shook our heads. Thatcher had an innate talent for research and detection which could but rarely be discerned from his actions, or distractions.

"They zombified him. Like the Tontons Macoutes used to do with their prisoners, you remember." Gus pursed his lips, as if such practices were beneath him. "Fugu poison, yeah. From a Caribbean fish."

"Haitian techniques are not often adaptable," said Gus. "It's a strange country."

"It's a rather outlandish thing to do, don't you think?" I asked.

"I didn't say it was done deliberately," said Thatcher. "This opens up all sorts of possibilities. Somebody more'n likely just screwed up."

"Then the doctors would have finished up the job in the back and sent the body on to Campbell's?"

"But they didn't," said Thatcher. "Maybe they didn't want to kill him. Maybe they *did* intend to zombify him, for whatever outlandish reason—"

"All entry points where his prints or eyes could be used to gain access have been recoded?" I asked.

"Yeah," said Thatcher. "He won't be much more use to 'em than a coatrack if they were going to try walking him up somewhere so he could get 'em in." Thatcher watched Gus shrug, and turn away. "Could be Jensen had himself taken care of. Could be somebody mistook him for someone else. Could be random and senseless, nothing more."

"Avi's been apprised of the situation?" I asked.

"Not entirely."

"Do Bernard and Susie know?"

"Told Bernard this morning," Thatcher said, toying at the edges of the note with two fingers. "You know how excitable's Susie's gotten herself about this. He's been talking to her about it while we've been down here, seemed like a good time to fill her in."

"Why are you letting me overhear all of this?" Lester asked. "It really seems like none of my business—"

"It's company business," said Thatcher, winking. "You're company."

"What do you trust me to do?" Gus asked.

"Don't take everything so personally, Gus," said Thatcher. "Everybody has an off day. Listen, go down there and talk to the doctors. If they don't spill by tonight, well . . ."

"Is the service over yet?" Bernard's voice broke in over the intercom, coming in as if on cue, seeming that he knew when best to enter for suitable dramatic effect.

"Come on down," said Thatcher, hauling himself upright. "Keep all this under your hat for the moment, Lester. We keep lots of little secrets around here, you'll get used to it. You have anything to add from what you've heard?"

"If the wound wasn't self-inflicted," Lester said, "I suspect it wasn't unwelcome."

Thatcher nodded. "If there's reason to this, we'll find it."

When Bernard returned to his office he entered without comment, took his seat behind his desk, and replaced his family portraits, shifting them again into their proper angles.

"What's eating you, Bernard?" Thatcher asked. "Have a good talk?"

"We made progress," he said. "I've been thinking that we should have Macaffrey's speeches written for him. We can't take the chance—"

"What're you talking about now?" Thatcher said, exasperated by Bernard's endless qualifications.

"I was reading the transcripts of the questions put to him earlier today," said Bernard. "It's worse than I imagined. If God speaks through Macaffrey, all I can say is He's a bring-down kind of a guy."

"You can't have a speechwriter for a messiah, dammit."

"Macaffrey," said Bernard, turning to Lester, "what's the purpose of the universe?"

"Purposelessness."

Thatcher shoved his hands into his pants pockets and glanced at the TV screen. Whatever presently played appeared so obscure in meaning that I believe even Bernard might have hesitated to attempt exigesis. Gus stared at all of us, wondering perhaps who was capable of the greatest betrayal. "Think of it as a matter of rephrasing," said Bernard. "He says one thing, we say another."

"What would you say about Mystic, Connecticut?" Thatcher asked. Bernard blinked his eyes as if worrying away a cinder.

"It belies its name," he said.

"In this note," Thatcher continued, " 'mystic' refers to Mystic, Connecticut."

"Does it?" Bernard asked, looking at him, and then at Lester. "Should you be discussing family matters around the help? Or did this conceit from beneath the stairs?"

"Mystic and Mahaica," said Thatcher. "Two ports. One importing, one exporting. Think New England's smuggling clams down to Rio?"

"If those two ports are involved," Bernard said, "a definite if, then any smuggling going on it would involve shipments of the product. Someone stepping into where we've left off."

"That's what someone's doing," said Thatcher. "I can smell it. Bringing it up from Bolivia in raw, maybe. Over from Colombia down the Amazon highways. Probably using those damn minitrucks to run the shift. Could we doublecheck those on satellite photos, see what's in the back?"

"With appropriate resolution we could count the change in the driver's pockets," said Bernard. "Say some operation along this line is ongoing. Should it matter at this stage? We don't have to keep that aspect of the operation going anymore, you've been saying that for a year now. Maybe it's some of the old Medellín boys have never quite given up —"

"They'd have been in direct touch," said Thatcher. "It's not them. And it's not amateur. Jensen wasn't running this, that's evident."

"It's certainly corporate," said Bernard. "Too many aspects of it are too senseless for it not to be. Whoever's involved here simply used Jensen as they'd have subcontracted any locals, here or there."

"My locals," said Thatcher. "Wouldn't mind getting reimbursed for all this free labor I'm probably providing."

"The operation isn't large or we'd have found additional traces of it by now," said Bernard. "It strikes me as test marketing."

"Then I reckon I know who's testing."

Bernard picked up the photo of his wife and pushed it an eighth of an inch to the left. "I reckon," he said. "Even if the Japanese are in it, Thatcher, what difference does it make? You claim we're getting out of the field."

"Drugs make the world go round," Thatcher said, shutting his eyes. "They need cash. Need to barter something other than electronics gear. If they're getting involved with the product, they'll start hauling in money and they can pick the market as they choose, long as we're not in it. Guess which market they'll take over if we get out."

"It would be preferable for Americans to be drugged with American drugs, of course," said Bernard.

"What if this Otsuka bird is behind it? I've only had a chance to look at this agreement once. Isn't there something in there about promising to support them in new Latin American ventures?"

"Purely pro forma," said Bernard. "We agree to discuss with them any proposals involving countries in this hemisphere before giving our approval. If we don't agree, we don't approve and they don't go ahead."

"This is some agreement you cooked up," said Thatcher. "Why do they want to sign it?"

"So they can get back to business, simple as that. Free up their assets. They've had to coast for too long—"

"There's another reason," said Thatcher. "And if Otsuka's big as you say he can't help but be in on this."

"Well, so we stay with the product and drive them out of the market," Bernard said. "But if you ever want this

97

damned computer to go online we need their assistance. Our boys can't take development further by themselves. We get them in on it as agreed and we're over the top. We don't sign, we don't get their help. I doubt we could pull off a kidnapping in that circumstance, so don't even consider it."

"Always good to keep all options open," said Thatcher. "You say Otsuka's pretty sharp?"

"He knows his yen from his yang," said Bernard. "You'd never guess. He looks like a root you'd find in a Chinatown grocery. Don't do anything to upset him, Thatcher. No confrontations, no escapades, no backup plans. He'll want to sign and he'll want to talk. Let him."

"Talk about what?"

"Whatever he wants. He likes hockey, talk about that. He loves old automobiles, flower arranging, bondage cabaret. He writes poetry." Thatcher sneered. "Talk about his grandchildren—"

"Grandchildren? How old's this guy?"

"Is it pertinent?" Bernard asked, smoothing the wisps of hair above his forehead down with a dry palm.

"Was he in the war?"

"Does it matter? We dealt with Griesing in Frankfurt all the time until he died last year, and we had substantial proof of what he had done."

Thatcher shook his head, as if by denying it he could even more assuredly swear that it had never happened. "Don't worry, Bernard. I'll handle it. You've seen me do it before. I'm taking Joanna along. It's another new project, after all."

"It'll be a shame to split them up, if only for awhile," said Bernard, suddenly staring at Lester and I as if he were a doorman and we, messengers. "They make such a cute couple."

Susie's voice cried out over the intercom. "Matters need attending, Bernard. I'm coming down."

"So keep Lester going through the preliminaries," said Thatcher. "Once I get a line on Otsuka I'll get a better idea of when we can start putting our teacher here to work."

"What are you talking about?" Bernard said, laughing, yet evidently finding little humor in what we said.

"Mystic, Bernard. Check it out."

As Gus prepared to leave, it occurred to me that he had, during the course of listening to conversation running around him, discovered the method of Susie's trick, one I'd often wished I'd been able to perform. Never one of the more approachable men I'd known, an almost palpable shell seemed to form itself around him, protecting as well as lending isolation and distance, protecting him from those he protected. He paused, standing by Lester, facing Bernard's desk.

"No one stopped you?" he asked Gus, pointing to the pen and pencil set's plastic knoll. Bernard stared at them as if watching a movie take an unforgivable turn.

"No," he said, seemingly completing the conversation we'd interrupted. "They trusted I had nothing to do with it." He left, brushing past Susie as she entered; she cringed at the feel of shell against shell.

"Bernard didn't know," I told Lester that night, in bed. "Thatcher told me he didn't. If he did know I don't think he wanted to be reminded."

"He doesn't seem to be a very sentimental person otherwise," said Lester.

"He is. And everybody had heroes."

"Does Bernard enjoy what he does?"

"It's grown on him," I said. "He's a natural at advertising. He started in product development but couldn't stand the sight of blood."

"Thatcher trusts him?"

"More than anyone except Susie, I think."

"What sort of relationship does Gus have with Jake?" he asked, after a minute or so more. "Besides that of a teacher?"

"Nothing abnormal," I said. "Avi once told me Gus wanted to get married and have a son. I asked him how he knew, and he said he could tell from Gus's handwriting."

"Did you want to get married?" he asked me.

"Once," I said. "Nobody wanted to go all the way."

Some did, truly, but that would have ruined it; I could never allow the men I'd loved the most to become my lovers. Genuine friendship between men and women was such a rare thing that to admit sex into such relations was unfailingly destructive, as if you were to carve your initials into a pearl.

"Lester—"

"Did you want to have a baby?"

"Not until I had him."

"Abortion's not illegal if you make enough money," he said, embracing me as if assuring that one of us would not abandon the other before the time was right. "We both know that. Why didn't you—"

"Thatcher's pro-life."

After Lester left I fell asleep and dreamed I saw his family's house. The ruin stood as desolate as an old English church, yet it couldn't have antedated America's Civil War; its stones could never have known the touch of a slave's hand. Attached to the chimney's outer wall was a bloody diadem, a rusted basketball hoop. Opening the front door I tiptoed in as if entering a nursery. No rags of memory clothed the room's nakedness; his house's amnesia was as profound as mine. I saw Lester standing in the kitchen. The pantry door was off its hinges and the room beyond appeared only recently unsealed. In the center of the far wall's fairness an aureola of punctures ringed an abyss blown into the plaster: an inoculation scar, the mark of an angel's bite, Saturn gathering his children around him.

—What happened to your family? I heard myself ask.

—Misunderstandings, his image said.

SEVEN

• • • • • •

Susie left the next morning for the Westchester estate, departing ahead of the others that she might oversee Thanksgiving preparations. Her personality's buds took full bloom, removed from Thatcher's shadow; Avi had heard that the year before two members of the kitchen staff killed themselves within a day of her arrival. Sitting in Bernard's office the next morning, waiting for Thatcher, I thumbed through the pages of her newspaper, seeing signs that the season was upon us. In Ohio a woman found her herald of the new millennium emblazoned in mold on the wall of her garage; analysts agreed that the stars proclaimed that stores remaining open would show profits this year; devil-worshiping cults were to be soon exposed in the north of England. There'd been a murder in St. Patrick's Cathedral: while confessing a venial sin, the confessant was overcome by the need to commit a mortal one, and so kicked his priest to death in the stall.

"Isn't Thatcher overreaching himself?" Bernard mumbled. Before I could answer, he responded, "No. Not this time," and I realized he was only voicing some mental catechism as he dallied over his paperwork. "What can he do to the Japanese except turn people against them?"

I threw the paper aside, having seen inspiration enough within to last a lifetime. Deciding to dawdle additional time away under the guise of work, I pulled a thick folder marked *Otsuka* from Bernard's outbox. Within were snapshots of the man taken years before, photos that by their angles suggested he had no notion that they were being taken. Pages of statistics referred to his businesses, his buyouts, his mergers and steals. I came upon some of his poems within, one of which had its lyric transcribed from Japanese into English.

> *They're on my nose now, inside of*
> *Twenty miles.*
>
> *Master arm on. Master arm on.*
> *Fox one. Fox one.*
>
> *God oh God.*
>
> *Good hit. Good hit on one.*
> *Roger that. Good kill.*
>
> *Good kill.*

"It reads like a transcript," Lester commented, studying the page from over my shoulder.

"No petals on wet black boughs for our allies," said Bernard, distracting himself from his unsolvables long enough to annotate. "He's fond of using found material in his constructs. Even in Japan he's quite askew from the norm."

"He seems almost interesting," I said.

"Thatcher would seem interesting, seen from Mars," said Bernard. "Otsuka's older, that's all, and he's had more time to elaborate upon himself. His followers worship him for having stayed alive against all odds." We might as well not have been in the room; Bernard was again transfixed by his desktop screen's fluttering green auroras. "Try not to evidence untoward fascination, Joanna, they've distractions enough."

"We're no longer involved, Bernard."

"You'll be involved, long as you work for him. I did forget we're playing minister and the choir girl for the nonce, however. Keep an eye on both of them, that's my suggestion. Prepare to duck."

"You're as paranoid as they are."

"With reason," he said. "Make sure the agreement gets signed. Progress on this computer is essentialed."

"Which computer?" Lester asked.

"You take an interest in technology? I'd imagine you'd think it superfluous," Bernard said. "As we apparently keep no secrets from you at present, I suppose I can detail a bit. Thatcher requires that a new super-super oversee company operations by the end of the decade; preferably next week. Without Japanese assistance it won't be done. Our team goes into conniptions working with fifth generation models. The masters from the east play with number sevens to unwind after drinking all night. Thatcher's logic is such that he believes if we combine the groups we'll shortly produce a number twelve, or what in theory is called, I believe, the Algorithmic Logistical Interactive whatchamacallit hoozis. How the language suffers at the tongues of these buffoons."

"A talking computer, I suppose," said Lester. "How'll it sound?"

"Mellifluous. Speaking only Latin for safety's sake, I'm tempted to say. It'll be a thinking computer, in theory. *Independent* thought. If it works as they believe it will, then

104

no one will ever need God again." Bernard forever pretended to recognize his social faux pas a beat too late. "Oh, Macaffrey, obsolescence hits everyone in time."

"This is what Thatcher wants now?" I asked. "Every time I hear it he's added a little more."

"It's Junior's backup, under any circumstance. A wise move, certainly. Where is Thatcher, anyway? Why isn't he down here yet?"

"He said he needed to brief the guards."

Bernard stared into his screen as if attempting to divine the future from entrails. "Stuff something in his mouth if and when he starts adlibbing."

Thatcher stuck his head through the doorway, giving us an impression of delight. "How's everybody this morning?" he asked, barreling in, clapping his hand on Lester's shoulder as if testing its friability. "What's the holdup? Can't sit around here all day."

"We *can't?*" said Bernard, harvesting folders from the fields of his desk. "Peruse the background material, Thatcher. You've seen the agreement you're signing, haven't you?"

"I'll wing it."

Our three guards trailed him into the office, each garbed in identical black suits with double-breasted jackets and baggy trousers, in toto resembling the fourth-string dance line at a deb ball. Jake scratched his nose, taking care not to remove any part of it with his still-attached scalpel. Avi, seeing Lester, allowed his eyes to lose their focus until they appeared to sink within his head. Gus's look held so little life I thought he might have had a dentist sever his facial nerves, so he would never again have to worry about giving anything away.

"Never felt so up," said Thatcher. "Had a hell of an appetite this morning. I could've et a dog—"

"Otsuka's not Korean, Thatcher," said Bernard. "Make do with sashimi. Go there, talk, sign, and leave. Simple?"

"It's handleable. Take care of Lester while we're away. Start pushing on that new info."

"Everything's under control," Bernard said. "What isn't, will be. Come back with the agreement signed—"

"Or don't come back?" Thatcher asked, laughing. "Don't come in your pants about it, hell—"

Bernard's blush was so intense that for an instant he could have passed as Susie's brother. "Some people are more useful alive, Thatcher. Remember that."

"We'll see how the jury calls it," he answered.

I never worried about Lester's safety when he left my house at night; in daylight, at Dryco, there seemed so much more to fear. He'd be with me that night, I knew all the same. As our quintet departed, Gus radioed the lobby before boarding the elevator, that multitudes might be warned.

"Dryden party descending. Please prepare."

Thatcher almost bounded off the elevator walls as we dropped to earth, in the cab's dim light appearing to toss off sparks. "They got the wounds," he said, chuckling. "I got the salt." Peering into the lenses affixed to the corners of the elevator's ceiling, he made faces, picked his teeth, slammed his fists against his enclosure. If I hadn't known he never touched the product, I could have only imagined that he'd done a snootful before allowing his feet to touch the floor that morning.

Jake dashed into the lobby as we landed, investigating all surrounding, sheer performance of his job sending him into paroxysms of mindless ecstasy not unlike Thatcher's. Our route to the exit transversed the breadth of the building's lobby and then the width of the outdoor plaza. Innumerable times Gus warned Thatcher that his chosen path was forever insecurable; hearing such truth only assured Thatcher that he should pass no other way. Gus snapped his fingers; lobby guards drew around us, shouldering guns and clutching long batons in their knobby hands. Once we exited, the guards formed two long unbroken lines, forcing hundreds of late-morning passersby into pedlock while we ambled to our car.

"Jake," Thatcher shouted ahead. "That guy. Watch him."

A man wearing a suit cut to appear as expensive as Thatcher's attempted to crash the line, refusing to break his stride for those either of heaven or of earth. As our barricade pushed him away he lost all reason, slinging his attaché case to the sidewalk, aiming curses at anyone near. When Jake approached he stepped forward again, leaning in between members of the line.

"Queer bastard!" he yelled, his tight collar buried beneath his billowing jowls. Spinning en pointe, Jake flung out his hand as if miming, for younger children, the sway of an elephant's trunk. The man tumbled onto the sidewalk. Thatcher, edging by, threw himself into the car; sinking into the back seat's leather, he breathed deep of the Siberian air within.

"Good to get out among the folks," he murmured. Gus sat next to the driver; Jake and Avi perched in the jumpseats facing us.

"Where are we meeting Otsuka?" I asked. Such details went unrelayed while they might be overheard and put to evil purpose.

"Midtown," said Thatcher, folding his arms before him. From the side of his mouth he spoke into the intercom. "How long till we get there, Gus?" Inches of lucite and steel separated our compartment from the rest of the car; Thatcher enjoyed pointing out that were we to be bombed, some of us could survive.

"Twenty minutes," said Gus, his voice crackling around us as it broke through the fuzz. "Depending on traffic."

Jake gripped the edge of the seat with his unapplianced hand so as to avoid being jostled to the floor as the car lurched across potholes, swinging north onto Broadway. Once the avenue ran one-way downtown from Columbus

Circle; Thatcher, surely for no reason other than to show that he could have it done, decreed that its traffic should race salmon-like upstream.

"What a wonderful world," he said, sighing, seeming so overcome by its beauty as to lose every remnant of worry and care. A riot was underway at the Federal Building, several blocks north of City Hall. Police restrained leashed Alsatians and faced a crowd of black citizens: front-line protesters wore knee-length coats; demonstrators in the rear carried signs, and clubs of impromptu design. GREENASSES OUT OF HARLEM, many of their placards read. Some of the others, ones hoisted by immigrants or the supporters of immigrants, demanded FREE BROOKLYN NOW. As we glided uptown, unbothered so long as we kept to our isolated center lane, the protesters moved in: those in the front pulled cats from beneath their coats and threw them onto the dogs; the others surged ahead, swinging.

"Can't depend on cops to do shit these days," said Thatcher, watching as if he was interested. "No excuse for it. Complain, complain, nothing those people've done for fifty years but complain—"

"It's their only right, Mister Dryden." Avi never feared putting his beliefs into words, knowing that no one who spoke freely could be harmed so long as words were flung forth without matching action.

"They got the right to work with what they're given," Thatcher said, concluding, "Hell. Didn't I?"

We bore north; Army vehicles headed south to balm the suffering they found. The turret of the lead tank swung right and fired at a News4 van parked close to the disturbance, bringing forth a yellow blossom that shot hot metal spores into the surrounding crowd. As our car rocked with the concussion I turned to look behind us; soldiers welled up from the skin of the tanks, raising their rifles, firing into the people blocks before the disturbance proper.

"Your news station, Mister Dryden," Avi pointed out.

"My Army," he said. "Joanna, you get a chance to look over the agreement?" I nodded. "You read the particulars? See anything funny?"

"Not at all."

With Thatcher's blessing the Army was at work farther north, constructing a concrete wall from river to river down the center of Fourteenth Street. They intended that each Manhattan neighborhood would thereby be better secured from agitators drifting in from other neighborhoods to assault the productive; to live thus would be no different from living in heaven, in a sense, where the quieting awareness of existing eternally beneath unblinking eyes was never forgotten.

"You think this will take long?"

"No," said Thatcher.

Throughout the twenties and thirties clusters of people bundled rags lay sleeping against the locked doors of vacant buildings; knowing a moment's peace, aware that few cared enough to harass them.

"Why do you hate the Japanese so, Mister Dryden?" Avi asked.

"What'd you say?" Words do stick, sometimes, if hurled at the proper moment. Thatcher was silent for a minute or two trying perhaps to rationalize an explication of beliefs never before challenged. "I'm sorry, I heard you. Let me try to explain," he said. "Two men want the same woman. She pretends to be indifferent to both of them. Till one comes out ahead she's not going to let on how she feels about the one who's winning. Might not matter to her which one wins." He sat forward in his seat, newly intent on his metaphor. "Does to them. Maybe they're old friends. Maybe they hate each other. Could be that if they hadn't fallen into the situation they'd never have given a good goddamn what happened to the other one. Give it time.

Soon enough they'll do anything to get the advantage. *Anything.* People'll do anything if they want something bad enough, period. I don't have anything against the Japanese. But they're there. They want my woman."

"What if the woman's indifference is genuine?" I asked.

"The fight takes on its own life," he said. "After a while she might as well not even be there. Love or business, politics or war, same difference in any situation. Sooner or later you'll be doing stuff you'll find painful to remember, later on. Stuff you won't want to tell your kids about. Do things you don't believe you're doing even as you're doing 'em. It's in the nature of the beast to do 'em just the same."

I could conjure in my mind an image of what West Fifty-sixth surely had been like when I was a child. Brick apartments, fifteen or twenty stories high, would have stood at the avenues; along the byway proper old brown-stones, converted livery stables, perhaps one or two small lofts would have covered the lots. Cheap restaurants and clubs would have frayed awnings extending to the curbsides. The shopkeepers of the street would know you as a customer as they'd known your mother; as they believed, and you believed, they'd know your daughter.

Otsuka's building, one of those architectural marvels that appear so sublime, alone upon the draftsperson's cold screen, took up almost the entire south side of the block. The tower, outlined with aqua neon, rose to unguessable heights; the upper floors were cantilevered over the lower, and so the street knew daylight for so brief a time at every noon that were the city to be abandoned, grass would have never sprouted between the cracks in the pavement. The atrium within was as tall as the building enclosing it; the empty elevators were as transparent bullets fired through long glass guns.

"He's the only one has an office in here," Thatcher said, eyeing the lobby guards within. "Check them out."

Gus identified our group; the guards directed us to enter the center tube, their voices carrying heavy accents. As they spoke among themselves they used a melodious Caribbean patois. Stepping into the elevator I saw that its floor was as clear as its sides. Gus stared at the ceiling, at the cables along the sides; I'd never realized that he was scared of heights. "I don't remember the Japs being real big on affirmative action," Thatcher said.

Upon leaving the elevator we emerged in Otsuka's reception foyer. The spoor of our own floor's decorators was present wherever we looked: there were curved charcoal-colored sofas, dusty rubber plants overgrowing their ceramic pots, nubby walls with the feel of a three-day beard. The seats of the sofas were cunningly tilted, so that those who waited could not linger long without sliding off. An HD monitor listed incoming figures from the Asian exchanges. The receptionist, a willow-thin Japanese woman, stood and bowed, something about her smile suggesting more of surgery than of training. When she spoke, her voice came from a place other than her mouth.

"Mister Otsuka expects you, Mister Dryden."

Taking a ballpoint from his pocket, he flipped it toward her; the pen flew through her image, bouncing off the wall behind. In the ceiling we discovered the lens that produced her hologram.

"They're getting good at this shit," Thatcher said. "We could put that to use somehow."

We stepped inside. Otsuka sat at his desk, his form silhouetted by the window behind him. His view was that of another window, across a space no wider than a tenement airshaft. Metal shutters veiled the opposite building's eyes. Japanese prints of traditional design were hung on the wall above a fireplace whose hearth seemed never to have seen a log. Upon his broad teak desk were a bonsai tree and a large amber lump; trapped within the amber was a tiny frog, preserved in mid-leap. Otsuka was as well-groomed as a dowager's corpse. His companions assisted him in rising, holding his arms when he tipped forward as if fearful that in bowing, he would break.

"A pleasure, Mister Dryden," he said, singing with ancient and unexpectedly resonant pipes. "Your presence is a great gift."

"Good, 'cause that's all I brought," said Thatcher, sweeping out his hand. "My associates."

"Mine," said Otsuka. His two bookends made their bows: they were mature men, with silver hair and rimless glasses; their tailored suits failed to hide their mass, and in the day's dim light they appeared to be carved from rock. All guards present sized each other up. "I am sorry Mister Leibson cannot join us today. We've worked so closely of late you will understand me when I say I sometimes think he must be one of my employees."

"I know the feeling," said Thatcher, rocking back on his heels as if preparing to swing. "He runs a one-man show in our operation. Keeps him busy."

"Sit, please," said Otsuka, fingering a chromium nipple built into his desktop. "Our meeting must be honored." A door that hadn't been there moments before slid open, and a young woman emerged, proving her existence by the silver tray she bore. From the tray she took a crystal decanter and thimble-sized cups. "A sixty-year-old single malt," Otsuka said. "Hard to come by."

"I'm not much of a drinker," said Thatcher, tossing his drink down as he might Kool-Aid. "From the Emperor's collection?"

Otsuka shook his head so vigorously that I feared his withered face might crumble away from his skull. "He abstains. A gift from the late premier," he explained. "Where is your wife?" Thatcher shrugged, holding his thimble up for a refill, behaving as he'd promised and not grabbing the bottle by its neck. "Mister Leibson tells me she is an active proponent of our renewed alliance. In the past I believe she has dealt with several political appointees, I should say, from my country. This belief in equal rights for those within equal classes is so peculiarly American, don't you believe? Even now in Japan the wife too often remains simply the pipeline between husband and children."

"That's what we got plumbers for, over here," said Thatcher. "She's good at what she does."

"Perhaps my lessers are correct, I fear, and women should be kept from participating in business. They are too good at outsmarting us. The lovely woman who attends you today." His young boy's eyes studied me as he exuded his opinions. "She is more than your secretary, but is not your *tayu*."

"We don't do those things here," Thatcher insisted. "Diseases, you know. Got to keep business risk-free, within reason."

"She would be your *miko*, then?"

"What is it?"

"Difficult to translate," said Otsuka, tapping his cheek with a thin finger, a bone sheathed in skin. "A shamaness of statistical productivity, in the sense I use it. One who blesses the shrine of capital."

"We got that covered, too," said Thatcher. "Joanna's too down to earth for that feminist mystic stuff. She oversees new projects."

"And I am a new project, true," he said. "Still, Mister Dryden, remember that defending the spiritual quality of your business is as important as having faithful *nihirisuto* to protect your personal well-being. Forgive me, please. When I am with Mister Leibson we speak my language as if we were friends. *Nihirisuto*. Laughing samurai, you might say. Dancers at the lip of the volcano." He examined our guards as if wondering how much they might bring. "In my youth I

113

kept with me always the long sword from Kyoto that Hiro now carries for me." The larger man, on his right, bowed lower; the scabbard's tip protruded from his jacket, obscene in its bluntness. "But these are the words of one who prepares to leave this world. There is no need to expend the declining energy I have when my associates may do it for me. In this setting, certainly, it seems so unnecessary."

"Seems so," said Thatcher. "Trust makes the world go round."

"And our countries have had so little trust in one another for so long."

"We'd've preferred to settle our differences sooner, certainly. But there's no sense running into anything till you've looked to see what you're running on."

"I wouldn't have expected you to put it any other way."

"Past few years, your country's had it hard," Thatcher said, failing to express in his countenance the semblance of sympathy he sought to give. "Your people, too. It's a shame."

"It has not been so difficult as some might have hoped," said Otsuka. "Persistence in the face of hardship is often rewarded."

"Often," Thatcher repeated.

"Still, through my foresight our industrial hollowing-out was nearly complete when this so-called Readjustment began. While we expected certain emergency measures on the part of your government, we did not foresee that the opinions of individuals would cause us to be treated as enemies. It seemed so much more unwise for you than to us, in a sense. The freeze on our assets hurt so many of your own countrymen, you know. America has been in such a perilous state since that time."

"The sensible man who's starving can always convince himself somebody else's hungrier," said Thatcher. "America's never been stronger than it is today. A little adversity builds a lot of character. Think I'm broken up about it? Aren't I smiling?"

"Mister Dryden, the adversity of others has built your character. Your strength-through-joy approach is something I put little stock in."

"Are you calling me a Nazi?" Thatcher asked; I prepared to do as Bernard demanded, and squirt in conversational lubricant, but had no chance.

"A witticism, Mister Dryden," said Otsuka. "In some ways Americans would be ideal Nazis, but in the long run it could never work. Every man would insist upon being his own Füehrer." Thatcher gripped the arms of his chair as if readying to leap up and strangle his proposed ally. "I mean no disrespect. Not everyone appreciates my humor, sir. That your Mister Leibson does counts for much in my eyes. He and I see things as they are. My countrymen neither appreciate my belief in the individual nor my telling them what they prefer not to hear about what they choose not to see. In America the concept of individualism is at least honored in theory. All I earlier intended to say was that our stasis was brought about by your decline, and neither of us need to have suffered so much. Nothing more."

"What I'm trying to say is we've finally got our house in order, and now we're ready to start helping the rest of the neighborhood—"

"The arsonist always returns to the scene of the fire." Otsuka held his hands before him, as if in prayer. "A new approach must be made by you first, Mister Dryden."

"What approach? What are you talking about?"

"Leaving aside nearsighted economic retributions," Otsuka said, "I have heard stories of how you refer to my country, and my people."

"What'd Bernard tell you?"

"Mister Leibson has been a model of circumspection in these matters, Mister Dryden. His view of all members of humanity is consistent. But a bad word shouted from a cliffside echoes off the rocks, and I have heard these echoes in several places."

"I'm not sure what you're getting at . . ."

"Have you not at times called us yellow perils? Whale eaters? Monkey boys?"

"People get upset and say things—"

"Japs?" Otsuka said. "Gooks?"

"My brother was in Vietnam," Thatcher said, as if that explained.

"I have never been in Vietnam, Mister Dryden. Only Americans go to Vietnam. Perhaps it would be similar, and more accurate, were I to call you a Nazi in such circumstance—"

"You all don't have any room to talk," Thatcher said. "Way you treat Koreans. The Chinese. Things you've said about American people—"

"I treat all equally, Mister Dryden. I have said no such things. The Japanese are a homogenous people, sir, but to remain that way we shot no Ainu from trains. We imported no Koreans to sell in our cities' markets. We never beat American students to death in our universities simply for being intelligent."

"You're still bad as we are."

"Ours are both racist nations, Mister Dryden. But we'll have none of it between us if you want my business. This is not in the agreement but must be agreed to. You will never call me or my people anything other than Japanese again, to my face or behind my back. Is that agreed?"

"You have to understand it wasn't deliberate," Thatcher said. "My dad was in the war."

"In the European theater," Otsuka said. "I was in the war, Mister Dryden. When I was taken prisoner it was by Americans considerate enough not to send my skull back to a girlfriend as a token of love."

116

"He could have been in the Pacific—"

"Then we might have killed each other, and where would we be today? Ours are different countries now than what they were. We must both remember that, and not view each other through our fathers' eyes."

When Thatcher at last replied I barely heard him. "That's true."

"To fruitfully share our hegemony," said Otsuka, "we must trust each other as partners, if not as equals."

"I can drink to that," Thatcher sighed. Otsuka smiled. "Let's do it, shall we?"

Otsuka pulled at the sleeve of his righthand associate. "Please hand the papers to Mister Dryden. Mister Leibson has gone over the working copy with you, of course."

"Of course." As Thatcher speedily read through the clauses, I relaxed, and allowed my glance to drift across the prints on the wall, assuming them at first to be Hiroshige's; noted in the corner of one landscape a pair of golden arches.

"Your hard bargaining may cause us difficulties in the future, Mister Dryden," Otsuka said.

"We'll be dead by then," Thatcher mumbled.

"The only way to offset the thirty percent share of our profits that you require will necessitate an end to the present deflation, true, but perhaps to too great a degree. Some of my advisers believe me foolish to make such a settlement."

"People'll have to pay what we charge, won't they?" Thatcher said. "Long as they got something to trade we can always work something out."

"Our retrofitted world cannot long exist on this barter system your country introduced—"

"It was my wife's idea, actually," said Thatcher, reading the pact as he might the lease for an apartment. "You all don't like it cause your money'll be going like everyone else's, once you get rid of what we turn loose, and you don't

117

have nothing left to trade but brains and VCRs. Nobody else complains."

"What choice do they have?" Thatcher grinned. "We are not so bad off as all that, Mister Dryden, and you know that."

"I got one question. This bit about programs employing viable personnel components of—what the hell? South-hemi states?" Thatcher reread what he'd quoted. "People of Latin America, I suppose. I'm curious as to what your intentions are for that part of the world."

"What is the context for your inquiry?" asked Otsuka.

"What're you going to do down there?" asked Thatcher. "Clear enough?"

"The agreement allows only for the discussion of proposed projects. Your approval is necessary for any actions taken after the date of signing. Otherwise, certainly, we would lose our favored status—"

"Actions already underway are unaffected?"

"Of course. Mister Dryden, you look upon Latin America as you might look upon your mother."

"I was reborn there," said Thatcher. "What sort of things you got underway down south?"

"Nothing unexpected. We possess a certain amount of liquidable property there as we do in many places. Money we once had that we were unable to invest in the United States had to go somewhere."

"I see."

"Mister Dryden, your doubts are still evident. For a moment examine your other partnerships and see the benefits of realigning with Japan. Who else is out there with whom you deal? Europe? Because of their own so-called alliance they believe they will shortly be able to dispose of us both. So they've believed for six years, and someday they may convince one other to believe. China? You don't nurse vipers without knowing they'll strike when they choose.

Russia." He paused; sighed, and rubbed his eyes. "Mister Dryden, your countries have an incomprehensible relationship. Each of your nations seems a dream of the other. This war without war the two of you have ongoing seems likely to bankrupt you in time, no matter the business you believe it creates—"

"We tried not fighting," said Thatcher. "Just didn't seem natural. It's not as if there're dangers involved. The Pax is signed, and in long-distance conflicts we both use local advisers—"

"So that your Army may be saved, to use in battling against your own countrymen. That is the most puzzling thing of all."

"This incountry stuff is penny-ante insurrection, that's all," said Thatcher. "Long Island wouldn't go along with the FEMA plan. Too many posses quartered out there weren't used to working inside any law." Most had worked for Thatcher; he never forgave. "You don't see martial law still in effect anywhere but here, do you? It's unavoidable. We're just mopping up now. I'll be on the winning side of the civil war this time, that's for sure."

"Your soldiers have been mopping for two years," said Otsuka. "Your Army cannot settle a disturbance among your own people not a kilometer from where we sit."

"There's just more of 'em out there than originally estimated," Thatcher said.

"I would say America should invest its capital and its young men in areas where they might have more purposeful effect."

"Well, it's our problem in any event," said Thatcher. "New York's got to be secure. We don't need Japanese help on that."

"But you do in other areas, Mister Dryden," said Otsuka. "You need a dependable friend."

Thatcher nodded to Avi, who handed him a fountain pen

with a golden nib. Upon signing the agreement he passed it over to Otsuka, who inked in his own ideograms.

"That our age may again know reason," Otsuka said. "As Adam Smith wrote, economic self-interest guided by the unseen hand of God enriches the marketplace."

"You got to watch out for that hand."

"Our new world," said Otsuka, reading over the signatures. "So much clay awaits its sculptors."

For several long moments Thatcher was unnaturally pensive, as if he already regretted having signed. "Sometimes it takes a while to see everything in the big picture," he said, wistfully, as if admitting to a character flaw. He folded his copy of the agreement into a neat square and stuffed it into his jacket pocket.

"Remember, Mister Dryden," said Otsuka, smiling, showing no teeth. "What you don't see is Japanese."

"We have to move," Thatcher said, standing, walking over to where I already stood. "You'll forgive us?"

"Of course," said Otsuka. Thatcher nodded.

"Go!"

Thatcher took me down with him as he threw himself to the floor. He lay on top of me; the rug's pile scoured my face as he shielded my head with his hands. Along with a cacophonous uproar I heard what sounded like the thunk of darts striking wood. Thatcher entered a state beyond consciousness, I sensed; as he heard each dart take its mark he thrust himself against me. Flattening my hands against the carpet I was able to lift myself up, rolling him off me before he could attain his ultimate joy. Standing, I saw that it was done. Jake squatted atop Otsuka's desk, between the bonsai and the amber, and Avi stood where he'd been all along.

"To the elevator," Thatcher whispered, wrapping his arm around me in pretense of concern as he got up, taking firm grips with his hand. Even his voice trembled. "Nice and calm."

All should have been confusion and blur, but each moment seared itself into my mind, so that even now I can call up each image of the afternoon as easily as I might find a photo in an album. Otsuka's associates bore the look of dolls tossed haphazardly against the spattered window, their arms thrown back, their heads dangling. Otsuka himself appeared to have fallen asleep while in prayer, having had no more time to wait for an answer. Gus had found his own rest upon the darkened carpet. From his angel's perch Jake stared down at his mentor, his face as livid as that of his friend's. Taking up Otsuka's sword from the desk, where the associate had dropped it unsheathed, he tied its strap around his waist; then he glared at Avi, appearing no less surprised than I to see him holding a gun.

"Nice and calm," Thatcher repeated. We drifted away then, floating across the office, into the reception area and past the ever-smiling receptionist into the elevator. I'd had dreams that seemed more real. My stomach burned as if I'd swallowed boiling water; I couldn't stop my hands from shaking, and pressed them between my arms so that the others wouldn't see. Feeling wetness on my face as if I'd run for hours through the rain, I watched seventy stories vanish beneath my feet as we plunged to earth. As we emerged at the bottom I recall wondering what else Thatcher had in mind; if another sudden episode was planned, simply to add a fillip to the fun he'd already had.

"Thanks a lot," Thatcher said to the guards gathered round the information desk. "Nice place."

None of the guards stopped us as we walked out the doors; no one stopped us when we walked on, to the car. No one would stop us once we drove away. A haze began to cloud over my mind, making each moment darker and ever-colder, but rather than being swallowed within white it was black that overtook me, black deep and limitless; as if, having been pitched from heaven into space's floorless pit, I realized too late that not even stars would keep me company. Awakening once more I found myself in bed, at home, later that night. My head reeled in unending implosions as I allowed my feelings to detonate. The last thing I remembered from that afternoon was Thatcher's voice, breaking as if with puberty, saying only *yeah*.

EIGHT

· · · · ·

"**I** hate to be in the same world with him," I said. Lester and I gazed out the living room window, through a lacing of dead branches toward the far-off river and the Palisades farther still. I'd never made money enough in my life to have paid for the drapes in Thatcher's house. "Not long after we started working for him I asked Bernard if he thought Thatcher was evil," I said. "He said it was like asking what jazz is."

"The mysteries come soon enough, Joanna," said Lester, an unexplainable cheerfulness hanging over him. Thatcher's own holiday glee so infused his spirit that the day before he'd unexpectedly invited us to this year's Thanksgiving celebration. We were driven up; in those days the Dryden estate consisted of a couple of hundred acres running east from the Hudson River. A high granite wall girdled every inch. The main house dated from the turn of the last century, and had twenty rooms; for so long as I'd known him he'd planned to raze it and replace it with something cozier. While spying Thatcher's bounty I eavesdropped on the comments of others who believed themselves to be speaking freely, as I knew few better paths to enlightenment in this world.

"Bernard told me not to worry about Tokyo," a man whispered. "Everything's under control."

"You see the face on that new bodyguard?" a woman asked. "The little faggot?"

"Psycho," said her companion. "Best kind to have, he tells me."

A waiter glided past us, proffering a salver heavy with stunted olives and Velveeta-filled chicken livers; we declined. "You heard the official explanation yet?" Lester asked.

"It's still in the oven, I suspect," I said. "Bernard must have taken the news better than I thought he would. I don't know what happened after they took me home Tuesday. Yesterday they were shut up in their offices all day. What tests were the doctors giving you?"

"I don't know if I passed," he said. "They gave me a Bible to read. Maybe to get the story straight."

"Probably want you to see what to avoid," I said.

"Why'd Bernard look so gloomy?"

"He and Martha usually spend Thanksgiving at home, watching the parade and having dinner afterward." Macy's —not part of Dryco—had announced that morning that they would no longer sponsor the parade, after that day's events; too many victims intended to sue. "Bernard once told me he'd come up here on Thanksgiving only if they served up Thatcher with an apple in his mouth."

"Thatcher needed him up here?"

"For punishment, perhaps. Doubtless we'll find out soon enough what's going on. He has something he wants us to do, I can tell—"

"Wants *me* to do," said Lester. "Why didn't Bernard's wife come along?"

"Martha refuses to have anything to do with Thatcher anymore."

"What'd he do to her?"

I shook my head. "Some people reach their limit sooner than others."

"Then these must know no boundaries," he said, regarding the crowd engulfing us. The house's rooms were not large enough to dwarf multitudes; the twenty-five present made the space feel as cramped as a subway car. They laughed and joked among themselves as if they were having a good time. "Who are they?"

"His closest surviving business associates," I said. "Us, Avi, Jake—"

"They have to work even though the estate guards are here?"

"Who else to guard the guards?" I asked. Since Tuesday Avi had avoided me as studiously as he'd avoided Lester, seeming fearful and ashamed. A third party negotiated for the retrieval of Gus's body, and so Jake went to Campbell's that morning before coming up, bringing along his own jar in which he could carry off the cremains. There'd been no autopsy; everyone knew how Gus died.

"Aren't there any family members?"

"Junior," I said. Thatcher Dryden, Jr. sat in a chair in a corner of the room, and could not have looked less comfortable had he appeared suddenly among a mixed populace in a strange city, naked and speaking a language no one understood. "I think he's fifteen."

"Seeing him I'd have thought he was a foster child," said Lester.

"His mother loves him, poor thing. He's more postliterate than Jake, I barely understand him when he talks. Susie insists he run the company eventually. Thatcher doesn't want him to. That's why he wants that computer in place."

"He's the only other family member here?"

"The only one alive," I said. "I don't know what happened to most of them. Bernard told me about Thatcher's brother once. He was older. He and Thatcher started the business, and then Susie came in on it. They took over the running of it after his brother was killed."

"What happened?"

"Medellín was involved, as I heard it. They'd been dealing with Cali and some argument developed, Bernard told me Thatcher opened his refrigerator one morning and his brother fell out. That inspired him to do whatever it was that he did to gain control of their operation—"

"What about Mrs. Dryden's family?"

"She had a brother. He worked for Medellín. They found out, after—"

"And Thatcher had him killed?"

"Susie."

A house guard loomed behind me, tapping my shoulder; I wondered if my fellow guests believed I let slip too many family anecdotes. "Mister Dryden wants to see you now," the lug said, then walked away. Taking Lester's hand in mine I walked him toward Thatcher's hall.

"They have family skeletons, rather than trees," I remarked. Jake idled in the approach to Thatcher's study, browsing over Thatcher's coin collection; gold doubloons and eagles mounted in framed panels hung above the wainscotting, and the sconces' creamy lemon light made the coins shine like miniature suns. I noticed the black mourning band Jake had tied around his sleeve.

"You all right?" I asked, stroking his shoulder; Jake never felt more than an animate assemblage of lumps. He nodded, blinking black eyes bright with red flecks. "You got Gus this morning?"

"Solo," he said. "Pickupped. Did the drop bridgeways. Ashes to ashes to ashes, full fathom five." He jerked his head toward the doorway and quoted from his assignment. "Shake off slumber, and beware."

Avi allowed us entry, keeping out of our sight as he opened the door, locking it behind us as we came in. There'd been six windows in Thatcher's study; he'd bricked them over and tucked the bricks beneath curtains. Redwood shelves sagging beneath the weight of thousands of old LPs lined the curtainless walls. Avi reclined on a black leather divan and concentrated his stare on a spot on the beamed ceiling. Bernard paced back and forth before Thatcher's desk, his movements recalling to my mind those of the polar bear once imprisoned in the Central Park Zoo, Thatcher propped his bare feet upon his cleared desk. Behind him were three filing cabinets kept forever locked, the ones that he claimed housed his most useful precautions. He spoke to me.

"Hon, you know how I hate to see people get all carried away by their emotions."

"You've carried me as far as I'm going—" I started to say.

"Have a seat, son." Thatcher tugged at Lester's sleeve, and pointed to a nearby ottoman. "You too, Joanna."

"Are you going to listen to me? You expect me to verify your account to Bernard? I'm not backing you up, Thatcher—"

"Bernard, haven't I been straight as a ruler with you?" I didn't look to see Bernard's reaction. "Moral support's kind of superfluous at the moment, hon."

"There's no excuse for what you did," I said. "None at all."

"Tell me, Lester," he said. "Does dining at the table of a murderer make the guest bad as the host?"

"Sometimes," Lester said. Thatcher shrugged, and held out his hands as if expecting to have them slapped.

"Smell dinner cooking?" he asked. "Hope you all went easy on breakfast. Got a treat coming up."

Bernard sighed, sitting down in a wingbacked chair, giving all signs of having paced himself into a stupor. I stood before them, anxious to bear witness.

"Even if you're blind to all others, Thatcher," I said, "don't you think you might watch out for yourself? Don't you think you could have been killed the other day? You think of that?"

"My boys don't miss when they aim," Thatcher said. Avi ignored the compliment offered, and examined his nails as if searching for lingering stains.

"It's insane, Thatcher. It's immoral. I've had as much of this as I can take—"

"We were so busy yesterday I never got a chance to explain," he said. "It'd be a natural feeling, thinking I've not been on the up-and-up about this—"

"Your explanations never explain," I said. "They rationalize, they make excuses, they lie. They never explain. What reason could you possibly have for murdering them except paranoia, Thatcher? You can't answer me, can you—?"

"Where have you been working all this time, sweetness, a convent?" Bernard said, interrupting. "None of this should be new to you, it's only your first direct experience. Every virgin suffers pain when the moment comes."

"It's been explained to your satisfaction?" I asked.

"The agreement is signed, after all. Shouldn't judge a book by its writer."

"Reality's a tricky business, hon," said Thatcher. "No sooner you get used to the way you think it's sitting than it flips right over on you. You have to be ready to jump before it does. Once we explain, you'll understand why there couldn't be any other response. You're sensible as Bernard is when it comes to cold, hard fact—"

"Your facts are slipperier than reality," I said. "And I'm not that sensible."

"You've tried to give the impression you are," said

Thatcher. "You're being as hard on me as you are on yourself, hon. That's not fair to either of us. What kind of heathern you think I am?" His face was angelic; his eyes, moist as a calf's. "Just a question of putting a chokehold on reality before it puts one on you. You got to try, 'cause if you don't, then you deserve to get anything life throws on you." He doodled on a pad as he spoke, marking out small circles and then slashing them through with x's. "That's the trouble people have when they're out on the edge. Stay out there long enough, you're bound to get cut at some point." He shook his head. "Most people can't bear the sight of their own blood. But once you get used to your own you don't mind anyone else's quite so much."

"There's no reason for any of it, Thatcher."

"Everyone has reasons, Joanna," said Bernard. "Every reason imaginable."

"A little background first," said Thatcher. "What's the rule of thumb interrogating those who won't give, Avi?"

"The thumbrule is that if the subject hesitates, the family will be lost," Avi said, reciting with less élan than had Lester's students. "If the family is absent, use their memory. If the family is present, work with them physically. If the subject is a wife, use the husband. A son, the mother. A father, the daughter."

"Monday night a father with daughters broke," said Thatcher. "One of the doctors spilled his guts, you might say. Seems our man Jensen is taking the air at Montefiore, up in the Bronx."

"What does he have to say for himself?"

"Ask the turkeys in the kitchen what they have to say for themselves," Thatcher said, laughing. "He's more than zombified, as it turns out. An irreversible coma. Doubt he's much for idle chitchat at the moment. Truth cries when it comes, all right. Now who do you think had him shipped up there? Old second gunman himself."

"Gus—?"

"Got in a little far over his head this time," he said. "After a while it must have affected his mind, having to keep new realities straight all the time. Working in Cuba but doing for America. Working in Mexico but doing for Cuba. Russia and Libya and Italy and who knows where else. To this day I don't think he knew who he was working for in Dallas, and would he have been surprised . . ."

"If he was even there," said Bernard, in a voice less direct than usual.

"He was there all right," Thatcher said, reaching behind him and patting his files. "I guess even you still have trouble sometimes with cold, hard facts." He winked at me. "In any event, it's to be expected he'd be prone to freelance when the right offer came along. Wonder now what else he got into we haven't found out about yet."

"The doctor told you Gus was involved and that's why you had Avi shoot him?"

"You think I kill people just 'cause I like the sound they make when they hit the ground?" he said, sighing. "Bernard, pick up on this. I'm going to get my throat so raw jawin' if I'm not careful I won't be able to eat my turkey."

Though I hadn't noticed before, I became suddenly aware that no one in the room but Lester would look into my eyes; my wishful thinking made me think that perhaps they could no longer bear to see what they saw reflected.

"We were told," Bernard said, "that the poison, while of Caribbean origin as claimed, was introduced into Jensen's system not long after Jensen arrived at Newark, more than likely by means of a needle jabbed into his neck. The poison was too dilute to have the preferred effect. Gus made a boo-boo, to be pithy about it—"

"No doubt you've inferred that he was hired by Otsuka for this?"

Thatcher's face lit up as if he were my father, and I'd told him I'd gotten all A's on my report card. "See how naturally this comes to you once you get the hang of it?"

"I insisted that Gus be kept viable for prolonged interrogation, to uncover such facts as we could and to try as well a new method the boys have been working on," Bernard said. "As I knew I would be, I was overruled—"

"We'd have never got anything out of him," Thatcher said. "Nobody ever did."

Bernard shrugged. "Could have gone through Jake."

"True . . ."

"Was Jake involved?" He couldn't have been, I realized; he was still alive.

"Ain't no mud on Jake's shoes," said Thatcher. "Gus had an eye for talent, I'll give him that."

"Even if Jake had been domesticated enough to participate in these shenanigans, there was no reason to involve him. It was a one-to-one action. The fewer to know, the better. As far as Jake knows, his teacher was killed in the line of duty. It's good for role models to illustrate the drawbacks as well as the benefits of a career."

"You knew about this Tuesday morning?" I asked Bernard.

"It's my job to know," he said. "Don't give me that look." His stare suggested to me that he'd long before decided I could never truly understand. "Gus's fatal error was trying to drag the doctors into it after he screwed up. He was apparently the one who conceived the brilliant idea of having them forge the certificate. They carried out his wish, signing that particular doctor's name, only later realizing that she was in no condition to see to anyone's death but her own."

"See what happens when you rush?" Thatcher said.

"If the intention was to kill Jensen," I said, "why didn't Gus finish the job?"

"They wouldn't let him," said Bernard. "Isn't that wonderful? That *our* doctors chose to abide by the Life Acts astonishes me. They've never shown themselves averse to circumventing these petty legalities in the past."

"Bernard," Thatcher interrupted, glancing at me, "that's touchy. Get on with it."

"By that point the corpus was in their care, and had been seen by too many. They had to do something. Afterward, then, Jensen sped northward on the uptown express, leaving behind only an officially recorded and duly vouchsafed death."

"Do you think Jensen actually said anything to Gus in the car?" I asked, trying to ignore Thatcher's apparent concern. "On their way over—?"

"Oh. 'Can you keep a secret?'" Bernard quoted, and laughed. "It's rare to come across people who can sound so much like a bad screenplay in such strained circumstance. He said it, nonetheless. Jake slid open the divider when Jensen collapsed, and he and the driver heard him say it."

"So what's the secret?" I asked. Neither answered. "Do you know? Does it matter?"

"We're working on it," said Thatcher. "Obviously he was ready to spill the beans to somebody. I'd like to think he intended to do the right thing and tell me. He sure wasn't working with Gus. Why would he have even brought it up, whatever it was, if he had been—"

"All inferences and select facts do, however, point to Otsuka's involvement," said Bernard. "We did trace the two individuals mentioned on the note discovered."

"Once we ascertained it was Mystic, Connecticut that was referred to." Thatcher reached over to shake Lester's knee until Lester grimaced. Had I owned a pet I'd never have allowed Thatcher to hold it.

"Didn't Gus search Jensen's apartment?" I asked.

"Police found the note at his sister's," said Thatcher. "Even a blind hog roots up an acorn now and then. Avi's investigating Jensen's apartment again tomorrow to see

132

what might have been overlooked. He lived up on the Concourse, didn't he?'' Avi nodded. ''I think it was his grandmother's place. I guess it was cheap—''

''You own the building, Thatcher,'' said Bernard. ''It was a perk.''

''What about those two individuals you mentioned?'' I asked. ''Where are they?''

Bernard coughed, and eyed his nails as he took his hand from his mouth. ''Shot while trying to escape, sadly . . .''

''Both of them?'' I asked. ''In both countries?''

''That struck me as kind of odd myself . . .'' Thatcher said.

''We're dealing with backwater elements in each port,'' said Bernard. ''It's to be expected. Corrupt officials are like cockroaches, you can't get rid of them.''

''But we've made a firm connection. Just haven't discovered the exact scale of the operation yet—''

''How convenient that the facts correspond so well to the theory,'' I said.

''Isn't it, though?'' Thatcher, as ever, pronounced *isn't* as *idn't*; certain speech patterns of his youth he deliberately retained, that those who didn't know him might be lulled into thinking that his intelligence was less than theirs. ''I had my hunches. You heard Otsuka the other day, Joanna. Calling me a Nazi. Making fun of America. His talk was all sugar when he wanted to sound sweet but you could smell the vinegar underneath.''

''It's evident now why he agreed so readily to that thirty percent cut,'' said Bernard.

''It is?''

''Rule of the agreement is that operations already in progress by one country won't be interfered with by the other,'' said Thatcher. ''Thanks to Jensen, they have an operation in progress. So if we try busting it up in the usual way they can cut the whole deal cold, and at this moment that'd give 'em the edge. They've already transferred their bank accounts over to Europe and back home, isn't that right?"

"And we can't take chances on losing access to those scientists, now that they're in our grasp," said Bernard, nodding in response to Thatcher's question. "Susie's flying out to Los Angeles tomorrow to meet them, in fact, to be assured that they come immediately under our supervision as soon as their feet touch earth."

"It's obvious that Otsuka could have lived with the compromises he made in order to get what he wanted—"

"Most people can," said Thatcher.

"Why couldn't you let him?"

"'Cause it's just as obvious who'd have been the next target after Jensen," Thatcher said. "Strike before the iron gets hot, I say. He popped Jensen before he could spill, but he'd have known I'd've found out eventually. There's a Judas in every operation. Shouldn't think he'd have risked it."

"Luckily for our agreement," said Bernard, "Otsuka may have been respected in his country, but there was no love lost among his folk. The problem with living successfully for so long is that after a time your enemies increase geometrically rather than arithmetically. We exchanged the traditional harsh words yesterday with his successors, and the agreement remains solidly in effect."

"Why wouldn't it?" I asked. "No one was hurt but Otsuka. You can't take your cut from underground activities, can you?"

"That's what we're looking into," said Thatcher.

"What are you going to do about it, then?"

"Hon, you're thinking like us now," he said, his smile so irrepressible as it was irredeemable. "This is where you two come in, truthfully. First, go up with Avi tomorrow to Montefiore and pay your respects to Jensen—"

"To bring flowers?" Lester asked. Thatcher stared at him

as he'd once stared at me, ignoring the sass, seeing only an evanescent fulfillment of every earthly wish.

"Gus may have been talking through his hat, saying Jensen looked like he was thinking," said Thatcher. "But if he is thinking, I'd like to know what about."

"If he is, I couldn't say, Mister Dryden," said Lester. "You expect too much."

"Maybe he wants to get something off his chest besides his respirator tubes," said Thatcher. "Joanna, you'll oversee this new project solo. Strikes me you're getting damn good, handling yourself in these situations."

"I can't, Thatcher," I said. "I won't."

"Oh, don't look at me like that," he said. "Lester, keep in mind Jensen's not technically dead. I'm not saying I'd be angry if you told me there was nothing you could do, but I think you're underestimating yourself."

"We'll have to see," said Lester. "What else do you want?"

"It's a funny old world," Thatcher said, leaning back, stroking the arms of his chair as if they were his wife's, or even mine. "All you can do to get out of it in one piece. Events so often occur beyond the control of mortal man. No one can predict where lightning'll strike, can they?"

"Thatcher," said Bernard, "speak English."

"Say something happened to Japan."

"What something?"

"A natural occurrence?" asked Lester.

"What insurance companies usually call an act of God, you could say."

"What are you talking about?" Bernard asked.

"It's been on the back burner. I've been theorizing."

"You can't be serious about what I think you mean—"

"Look at it scientifically," said Thatcher. "As I understand it, Japan's a volcanic mountain range rising out of the sea, right in the middle of the earthquake belt. That so?"

"You want me to sink Japan?" Lester asked.

"You didn't hear me say that, did you?" he asked. Butter wouldn't have melted in his heart. "Hell of a concept, isn't it? Kinda get back at 'em for Pearl Harbor."

"You're losing it, Thatcher," said Bernard, brushing stray hair toward the crown of his head, as if to keep his skull warm. "I'm not hearing this. I'm not."

"Shit happens," said Thatcher. "Who'd lay the baby on our doorstep?"

"Macaffrey couldn't bend a fork using both hands," said Bernard. "He couldn't make dice move if he threw them. Now you want him to perform exploratory surgery on the eastern hemisphere? It'd be funny if I didn't understand your intentions. Haven't you learned anything? We have to get along with them, Thatcher—"

"Long as we've got Lester here, won't hurt to see what might be done . . ."

"I'm not going to listen to this."

"You ever read that boilerplate in the agreement you drew up? Either country can take over the other's business affairs in the event of nationwide catastrophe. There's our loophole—"

"Thatcher—"

"We'd be helping 'em out, that's all. Taking control of their operations for a spell, like it says we can do. Till they get back on their feet." Joy so enriched his voice that a singsong quality entered it as he continued to speak, as if he were crooning a child to sleep. "If there's anyplace left to stand."

"Psychosis I can deal with, Thatcher, I can't handle insanity—"

"You think you can have countries destroyed at your request?" I said. He regarded me as if I'd told him the sun rose in the morning, thinking it news.

"Subtlety's everything," he said. "What I think's unimportant, hon—"

136

"Enough of this," Bernard said, rising and walking to the door. Avi stood, blocking his exit. "Take a stress pill, Thatcher. Collect stamps. Do something to get your mind off things. We have enough to deal with as it is. Avi, unlock the door."

Avi looked to Thatcher, who gave his assent. "We'll be getting up ourselves in a minute. Almost suppertime. Can't wait."

Lester showed no greater loss of aplomb over this turn of events than he had during any other. Thatcher studied him for several wordless moments.

"Yes, Mister Dryden?"

"Thatcher," he said. "Thatcher, please. What do you think, Lester? You don't have so negative an attitude about this as Bernard has, do you?"

"Godness sent the rainbow," said Lester. "God brings the fire."

"Don't know as how I follow what you're getting at."

"Sometimes a challenge is taken up with interest," Lester said. "It's best not to offer such—"

"Who's challenging?" Thatcher asked. "An idle thought, nothing more."

"They'll see it as a challenge," Lester said. "As I understand the arrangement, that is. I couldn't guarantee what form Their response might take."

"Can't tell till you try, Lester," said Thatcher. "Christmas coming up. I love surprises."

"So does God."

NINE

● ● ● ●

Thatcher bade that we follow him into the living room; we hung back as he strode forward, hoping to lessen among the others the impression that we were with him. His appearance among the guests stopped their conversation cold; lifting a hand as he sauntered in, he signaled to all that his presence should neither distract their attention nor hinder their fun. As the guests picked up their words from where they'd dropped them, an almost palpable difference was noted in the volume and tone; a hitherto undetectable air of false nonchalance sharpened the now-subdued chatter, as when in a crowded subway car a lazar pushes suddenly down the aisle, thrusting a cup beneath willfully blind travelers.

"Boy," he said, noticing his son on the edge of the sofa, drawn deep within himself. "Get up and circulate."

Junior shook his head; such color as he possessed left his

face. Thatcher walked over, gripped him by the shoulders, and snatched him up as he might a misplaced cushion. Marching him across the room, Thatcher inserted his son into a close circle of acquaintances with the manner of one driving an axe into a pie. No sooner had Thatcher moved on than Junior fled the group, flying back to his nest, brushing his arms with his hands as if to preen himself, fearing perhaps that his brief exposure might have left spores of contagion behind.

"He has so much money," Lester said, admitting unexpected awe. "So much must go to taxes—"

"Thatcher and Susie are exempt," I said. "Dryco, the company, is exempt. I'm not, Bernard's not, no one else working for them is—"

"How?"

"Part of the deal," I said. "Last year the IRS actually sent someone over to audit him. Someone made a boo-boo, as Bernard might say. Gus showed him out."

"Bernard might say about what?" Bernard asked, rising up behind us as if from a cloud, clutching a drink. On the side of his glass was a cartoon of a turkey wearing a Pilgrim's hat. I couldn't remember the last time I'd seen Bernard drink, but knew I didn't want to recall. "Try as you might, you couldn't make it up. God must have made man in His own image, it's Thatcher's only excuse." Judging from his breath it was evident that he sipped from a refill. I wished he'd go away without my having to ask. "Have I offended sensibilities again? Silly me . . ." he said. "Sweetness?"

"You didn't care if I knew beforehand?"

"Of course I did," he said. "You might have given away the game, had you known. Your poker face won't get you through the ante."

"I could have been killed."

"You could have been. You weren't. God has mercy on us all, doesn't He?"

His preoccupations were writ plain on his face; I let what he said slip away from my mind. "You believe these plots of his?" I asked. "With Otsuka? With Gus?"

"There's evidence, Joanna. If he hadn't shown me the ground of being for his beliefs I'd have never gone along. Sweetness, it's not professional to take this so personally—"

"Oh, fuck you, Bernard."

He lifted his glass; took a long swallow. "In dreams," he said, his voice trailing away.

"Thatcher means what he says?" Lester asked. Bernard examined him as he might a spider crawling across his desk.

"Depends on what time it is," he said. "Or the phases of the moon. Barometric pressure. Says about what?"

"Sinking Japan."

"I was never consulted on it."

"Do you think he's serious?" I asked, and watched as Bernard's expression sagged from grim into chopfallen, as if he were disappointed in me for having needed to ask.

"Apparently. Concern as to the little yellow people is still evident. This too, will pass. Excepting Susie D, his infatuations linger no longer than spring rain." He raised his hand, and pinched Lester's cheek. "Some, sooner than that. It'll pass. Everything passes . . ."

"He should consider what he asks for before asking," said Lester.

"I've said as much." Bernard drained the remainder of his drink, letting the cubes slam against his lips, as if to punish in the midst of comfort. The ensuing pause held a deeper silence than one employed entirely for dramatic purpose. "Why would you care? You can't supply it, whatever he wants."

"Bernard, go away," I said. "If you're mad at Thatcher, don't take it out on us. I'm not sure why I'm even speaking to you, considering—"

"So don't." Turning from us he stumbled off, ambling toward the bar, giving signs of being embarrassed for what he'd later have to say.

"Bernard," I said, calling after him. He lifted his hand as if to shoo me away. *"Bernard!* Dammit—"

Lester moved closer to me, and whispered in my ear.

"Are you scared?"

"No," I lied.

"Me neither."

"It's unavoidable?"

He nodded. I slipped my arm through the crook of his, so that whichever of us was most tired might be supported by the other when we fell. With as little warning as when he entered the room Thatcher reappeared, throwing open the dining-hall doors and shouting:

"Happy holiday!"

The long table was so laden with tureens and casseroles, baskets and boats and bowls that the lace tablecloth was but barely visible. Between the candlesticks were five domed silver platters. The guests stampeded for their seats as if they'd been released from the starting gate under threat of fire.

"Don't shove," Thatcher said, failing to calm them. Susie rested, sipping from a tumbler, presiding over her side of the table, her duties of overseeing the galley slaves attended to for another year. Thatcher sat on her left, at the head of the table; Junior sat to his left. The room's high windows along the west wall allowed in late afternoon sunlight enough to wash every guest in gold.

"Everybody gets a drumstick this year," he said. A quintet of servants raised the domes, exposing the entrée. Some of the younger children present started to cry; of the adults, all were too overcome to speak, save Thatcher. "Don't thank me. Thank the boys at Perdue. We've got the lead in genetic engineering now. Europe can go hang."

Each nut-brown carcass bore six drumsticks. A vision entered my mind, a scene revealing a parallel world: Squanto presenting Miles Standish with giant roasted spiders, welcoming the immigrants to American shores. The sails are ordered raised on the *Mayflower*, and the fresh green breast is left to its lessees.

"How do they walk?" Bernard asked, raising his drink as if to salute. If he'd imagined that liquor might still his tongue, he had no one to blame but himself.

"Don't think they ever leave their pens. I look like a farmer?" Thatcher tapped his spoon against his plate as if to make it shatter. "Those of us who are still alive have a lot to be thankful for. A moment of silence, please, for those who've eaten their last piece of pie." Hardly had we bowed our heads before his benediction continued. "A couple of years ago, I don't have to tell you, we were facing a gloomy forecast. Look around you today. Business in every area up three hundred percent." To ascend from nothing was guised, as ever, as achievement. "The troubles across the river are just about thrashed out. The new alliance you all've heard about with our Japanese brothers is signed, settled, and in effect."

Polite applause of the sort that accompanies an announcement that the recording secretary is retiring followed. Two dozen chairs creaked, and creaked again; no one could eat until Thatcher finished his spiel.

"In finding the future, let's not forget where we left the past," he said. "Let us remember the Pilgrims, who, in looking for a better life, landed at Jonestown—"

"Jamestown," said Susie.

"*Plymouth!*" Bernard said, his word exploding as he corrected his masters.

"Wherever the hell they landed," Thatcher continued, "it was a stern and rocky shore, and they were comforted then as we are ourselves, by our wealth of spirit and by our families—"

"Speak for yourself, John Alden." We didn't have to look to see who said it.

"What did they do when they landed?" Avi asked, shilling at an instant's notice; another requirement of the job.

"They ate, because they were hungry," Thatcher said, his mood for oratory dwindling. "Thanks, Lord." The ceiling, firstly, was blessed by his gaze; then he turned his eyes to Lester, anxious to cover all possibilities. "Let's eat."

Perhaps I had no appetite anymore; the turkey could have been smoked cotton, for all it held in taste or texture. I declined a drumstick, that another might be doubly sated.

"Thanks for seeing to dinner, darlin'," Thatcher said. Susie smiled and nibbled cottage cheese, taking one curd per bite. The strict diet she followed, that year, allowed her only white food; on her plate were several shades of pale, those of unflavored yogurt, cauliflower, cave-grown asparagus, and mashed potatoes. Most seated gourmandized as if they hadn't been fed for weeks. Neither Bernard nor Lester seemed any hungrier than I. Jake extended his scalpel, lifting his cup of tea.

"Dad," Junior said, looking toward his father, and not at him. "Bread me."

Thatcher stared into the middle distance, as if spotting an unlikely mirage. "Bred you to speak English," he said. "Want to try again?"

Junior's lips moved without accompanying sound; the impression lent was that he'd had his voice erased, and didn't realize it. "Bread, Dad," he repeated, attaining audibility. "Starching's essentialed."

"For shirts," said Thatcher. "You want biscuits?" Junior must have twitched even in sleep; for an instant he drew mimosa-like from the table; then, catching himself in the act of showing weakness, quickly leaned forward, bumping his chest against his plate, knocking his plate against his glass. The glass spilled, soaking the tablecloth. A servant appeared, blotter in hand. "You got to be literate in the business world," said Thatcher; I could tell by his expression that he was trying not to laugh. "You ever going to understand that?"

"World's postliterary, Dad—"

"Listen to Bernard when he talks," he said. "There's talking for you. One of these days you're probably going to be his boss, and how's it going to look if your subordinates sound better than you do?"

Bernard dropped his knife and fork onto his plate, his efforts at eating ended. He said nothing that I would have hoped he might say.

"Understood, Dad. Doubledone. No ifs or maybes."

"You fucking idiot," Thatcher said, rising from his seat, as if to take better aim. "Here's your goddamn biscuits. Don't bother to ask next time if you're not going to ask in English." He slung a wicker basket top-heavy with rolls toward his son; Junior threw up his arms to ward off the blow. The rolls shot through the room, bouncing off the table, the walls, off the other guests. No one but the Drydens behaved as if anything were amiss. "How the hell'd I wind up with a goddamn son so goddamn stupid he can't even talk good English?"

"Shut up, Thatcher." When anger rushed into Susie's spirit, her voice lowered until she sounded as if she'd been born to broadcast. "Won't you ever let him be?"

"You can only baby him so much. He's going to have to find out what a tough world this is, darlin'. He can't be as stupid as he looks—"

Junior could bear his parents' opinions no longer; without a word he leapt from his chair.

"Where you think you're going? Come back here, goddamn your ass—"

He tripped before he'd gone five feet, falling into one of the immovable house guards stationed around the table.

Junior punched the man in the sides and stomach, flailing his fists to no evident effect; then, he dashed from the room.

"You have to speak to him in public like that?" Susie asked; anger increased her hunger, and her rate of intake, and within moments she was spooning food into her mouth as one starving. "In front of these people?"

"You're smothering the little bastard, darlin'," said Thatcher. "Mark my words, he'll turn out funnier than he already is 'cause of you, you can bet on it—"

"Well, he won't be like you—"

"What'd be the matter with that?"

"Just shut up, Thatcher, please shut up—"

"If he just talked normal like a normal person—"

"It's fucking Thanksgiving, Thatcher, so shut the fuck up—"

"I know my holidays," he said. "Don't you be telling me to shut up—"

"I'll tell you—"

We waited to hear what she threatened to tell. An aphasic look passed over her face, as if she was unable to say what her brain insisted she should relate. Lifting her chin as if for a facial exercise, she rubbed her neck; pushing herself from the table, Susie slapped her knees with her hands in an offbeat rhythm. When she coughed it came without sound.

"Darlin' —?" Thatcher asked, staring dumbly at his wife; she pointed to her throat. "Sue—?"

"She's choking," Avi said. No sooner had he said it than he reached her, lifting her from her chair as she slumped. Encircling her waist, clasping his hands across her stomach, he shoved up and in, attempting to dislodge what she'd aspirated.

"Help her, dammit—" Thatcher shouted.

Susie flopped in Avi's arms as if she were stuffed with rags; closed her eyes, holding in tears, and showed no signs of recovery. Thatcher jumped from his seat, and, without warning, began hitting Avi in the face, seeming to have decided that it was his fault that she so suffered, his frustration total, his rage absolute, screaming without words, slapping as Avi squeezed. Cuts opened above Avi's eyes; blood reddened the corners of his mouth, and I turned away. Avi seemed oblivious to Thatcher's blows as he undertook his work; appeared almost at peace, as if he felt he was receiving the payment he deserved for all that he had done.

"Get away," Thatcher shouted, shoving Avi aside, embracing his wife in his own arms, applying so vigorous a grip as to lift her feet off the floor. Her purple lightened with gray undertones. As they grappled there without sound I thought how like some private drama glimpsed briefly through a window in the night the scene seemed to be; by the crowd's noise I gathered that they were not so detached as I.

"She's dying—"

"Oh, God, Susan—"

"Help her."

Her arms dangled, her fingers snatched at air, her toes turned inward, brushing against the floor. A feeling as reprehensible as it was human entered me, and at that moment I knew I would be glad to watch her die; that I could have no trouble hearing, no problem forgetting, this scream in the night. Then, awakened as if by a siren's sound, I felt Lester take my arm.

"Together," he said, without speaking. "It has to be. Come on."

As in a painfully clear and fully recollected dream we glided across the room. Thatcher held his wife closely, as if to keep her soul from escaping; he'd so exhausted himself that we had no trouble pushing him gently aside. We lay Susie down upon the floor; Lester knelt before her, between her legs. I took my position behind her, propping up her body, putting my arms around her waist, clasping my hands beneath her heavy breasts.

"Close your eyes," Lester said, placing his hands upon her temples. Her perfume was sharp in my nostrils, a fragrant blend of spice and oranges, a clove-stuffed potpourri worn as if to ward away the plague. My hands grew ever-warmer as I pressed them into her flesh; warmth rose through my arms, over my face, sent a column of fire rising up my spine.

"Push," Lester said. Without warning my memories burned through my walls.

—*Push.*

The smell of cloved oranges suffused the ward's antiseptic air, overcoming alcohol's refreshing sting when I inhaled, holding open my mouth as if I were drowning, and wished to sink all the sooner. The hospital room's lights were so bright I thought they must be trying to set my eyes aflame, so that I might never speak later of what I saw. When I moved my head, first to one side, then to the other, I glimpsed my face, framed by askew halos, reflected in surrounding mirrors. Susie readjusted me, taking hold of my head in her hands, turning my face toward hers. My eyelids seemed weighed down with lead; as she kept her unwavering watch over me I believed, looking up, that she had been suspended from the ceiling, and wondered why.

—Push, Thatcher said.

—Like a train, Gus said. Breathe in. Out. Gets air in the head.

—Push, the doctor said.

Susie held me firmly, as if suspecting I might try to turn my head too quickly, and so snap my neck: offering no consolation, whispering no assurance, she took rather than brought, comfort. I couldn't see what was happening; the notion came to me that they'd decided to dissect me, for want of better to do. Glancing toward my feet I found that I couldn't see them; my legs served as framework for a snow-white tent; heads bobbed beyond its peaks, as if an encampment were climbing in. Susie pressed her hands against my skull. I began not to notice so much, after that; the pain elsewhere grew too great. My thighs shivered with the touch of chilled metal; I imagined them taking up shards of shattered mirror in order to scrape me away.

—Push.

A baby, I thought, realizing I was pushing without thinking; though I couldn't feel my body I felt too well the pain. I'd never known how large the smallest baby might feel. My pelvis seemed to be coming apart; I clenched my teeth together, wishing I had something to chew. Looking up, I stared directly into Susie's inverted eyes, so black and still that they could have been shaped from obsidian. I hurt all the more, once it was done.

—A boy, I heard Thatcher say.

—Competition, said Susie.

"Push."

Opening my eyes, feeling her shivers as she rasped out an unending cough, I allowed her to pull away. Blots of wet potato smeared Lester's shirtfront. He fell to one side; blood streamed from his nose and he lay on the floor hyperventilating, shaking as if too much voltage had shot through him. Thatcher helped Susie to her feet; I crawled over to Lester, gathered him up and cradled him in my arms, pressing my hand beneath his nose to halt the flow of blood. What remaining sense of time I retained disappeared as I sat there holding him; I would have been content to remain as we were, frozen in our pose unto eternity.

"Mother," he said, seeing me, not seeing me. I smoothed his hair; a moment longer and the bleeding stopped. Thatcher and Susie made noises that could have been those of laughter or of tears; I couldn't tell and had no desire to look. That I could be, in these circumstances, a bringer of life struck me as being incomprehensibly unfair, knowing as I did that having stolen one person from the grave, I'd allowed another to be led closer to his own.

"You okay?" I whispered. He nodded, not opening his eyes, resembling a newborn kitten as he lay there. The room's silence jarred me into more mundane consciousness; raising my head to see where everyone had gone, I saw them all still there. They stared at Lester; even Susie looked up from her husband's bosom long enough to glance our way, as quickly turning back toward him, her features holding as much of anger as of shame, and not a sign of gratitude. I could only imagine that, having seen the face of her angel of death, she recognized it as one she'd known all along.

"God bless," said Thatcher. "God bless us. I was right, Susie, I was right. Wasn't I? I was right. God bless—"

"God damn," Lester whispered, so that only I could hear. Bernard edged closer to us, holding his drink, keeping his distance, his face no less pale than Lester's. He looked down upon us as if from a mountaintop, for the first time since I'd known him seeing through me as he stared at another.

"Hallelulah," Bernard said. If I hadn't known better I'd have sworn he understood.

That night, later on, Lester and I talked our hours away.

"Everyone does have their reasons," he said. "As do They. It scares Them as it scares us."

"Why have I stayed there as long as I have?" I asked.

"Where would you have gone?" We lay in darkness in my lightless house; we didn't have to see each other in order to talk. "What would you have done?"

"I know now what I could have done—"

"You didn't then," he said. "Don't let blame lay its head in the wrong bed, Joanna."

"There were things I could have done," I said. "That really is the greatest sin. Seeing evil and doing nothing."

"Children learn their parents' sins better than their virtues," Lester said. "We should expect no more from Them than They expect from us. Only once will change come overnight and until that day comes you have to fight as you can, when you can. Until then, you get by."

"You almost sound like Bernard."

"Even a blind hog roots up an acorn, now and then."

"I've spent years trying to be like him," I said. "Like the Drydens. I shouldn't deserve better than they deserve. Avi knows that, he's accepted it. You saw him this afternoon—"

"He does as he does for different reasons," Lester said. "Why are you so hard on yourself?"

"I've always thought someone should be," I said. "I wanted her to die. For what they did."

"A human response to human acts. It's understandable."

"Not to me," I said. "Not now, not anymore. Not to me or to you or—"

"Understandable to Them," he said. "Joanna, the godlike in humanity is bad as well as good, and the evil that lives in people more than meets its match in Theirs."

"That's no excuse," I said. "I've brought so much of this down on myself. Some of my friends always said I must be an emotional masochist—"

"Most people are," he said. "I suppose I am. Don't you think a certain masochism is essential in a messiah? A certain sadism on Their part is sure unavoidable."

"But now I see how much I could have done differently—"

"When he was alive the other afternoon Gus told me something," Lester said. "He believed that if he hadn't gone to the knoll that day history since then would have been very different. Therefore he thought he was the one to bear ultimate responsibility for why the world is the way it is, today."

"He told you that?"

"In so many words."

"What did you say?"

"I asked him if he wasn't unsure whose shot was truly the one that killed. That it could have been Oswald, after all. He told me, it didn't matter, he was there, he could have done something else. The more he talked the more it became clear to me that he was as troubled for having to bear the guilt without receiving recognition as over anything else. I told him that as far as I understood it, neither he, nor Oswald, nor even Kennedy could have been there and everything would still have happened as it did. That didn't improve his mood. I suppose I could have predicted that."

"If so much is predestined by Them why do They give us what we perceive as free will?"

"It is free will as to how we get there. It's all in the perspective. It's more worthwhile to consider how much worse it all could have been."

"How?"

He had no answer; I suspect he knew, but saw no need to say. "What did the Drydens do to your baby, Joanna?"

"I don't want to think about it—"

"You thought about it earlier today," he said. "The baby was unplanned?"

So much of my life seemed to have happened so long ago, in another country, to another person, as I supposed it had. As I grew older the sense of disconnection pervaded my spirit, the feeling that moments existed only as they occurred; when certain stray memories eked their way into my soul they were, to a point, easy enough to slough off as nothing more than vague recollections of shows once seen, of books once read. Only when my guard slipped accidentally, as it had that afternoon, or deliberately, as it did now, could I relive a life consciously lost.

"I'd broken up with Avi but hadn't told him yet," I said. "About the same time Thatcher had to go on a business trip to Buenos Aires. Bernard wasn't able to make it. I was sent in his place. I'd only seen Thatcher once or twice before then, and never for so long a time. During the flight down he noticed me, I guess. He fished with all his lures. He seemed so different then, so charming, so—"

"So he hooked you," said Lester.

"At forty thousand feet," I said. "I'd come to suspect that I was sterile, but I wasn't. At first I thought I could get an abortion. The only way I could have made the connections was through Thatcher, and he wouldn't hear of it, as I've said—"

"He knew it was his baby?"

"There was the possibility it was Avi's," I said. "A fifty-fifty chance."

"He knew that." I nodded. "And Susie?"

"Nothing happened when she found out, which surprised me. I'm not sure how quickly she noticed the relationship. She was always running around doing something and at that point Thatcher was still subtle about it. The longer I was pregnant the more I wanted to have the baby, whosoever it was. By the time I went into labor I wanted my baby so much. I'd taken such good care of myself, I quit smoking, I didn't drink—"

"What happened?"

"They'd told me. Thatcher told me. He said He'd see to it that I had the best doctor in the company. I wanted a natural childbirth and he said no problem. Gus was my Lamaze partner. We'd practice in the office at lunchtime. They took me to Beekman when it was time. Susie and Thatcher and Gus. Avi knew I was pregnant but I swore I'd had the test and discovered it wasn't his, and I hadn't, I didn't want to know. I didn't want to lie to him and I lied just the same."

"Then?"

"They put my gown on me. Stuck something in my arm while they were—" While they were shaving me; while

Thatcher shaved me. He'd asked if he could, and no one minded but me. "I was so doped up. I remember lying on the table. I remember having my baby, and then I passed out. That's what I remembered—"

"I know."

"When I woke up again it was in recovery. I was the only patient. Thatcher was there. I asked him where my baby was." I paused. "I never even got to hold him. Thatcher told me later it was Susie's idea. At the time he just said shit happens. She'd insisted, he said. They didn't want to let me see him but finally did. He was all wrapped up. He had dark hair, like Avi."

"Did he say why—?"

I shook my head. "Maybe just for the hell of it. I don't know."

I started to cry, and then I couldn't stop; he held me, and I sobbed without ceasing for most of the rest of the night. No sooner had my memories bolted than I at last locked the door behind them; their odor would forever cling, their prints still scar the places they'd been.

"How could I do what I've done?" I finally asked. "I stayed with them. With him. How could I do that—?"

"If you can't say," Lester said, "no one can."

We lay there without speaking for long minutes after that, watching the room appear around us as dawn approached, lifting the veil from a new day's darkness.

"Joanna?"

"What?" I said, barely hearing myself

"Even when people try to do right it so often turns out wrong. It's in the nature of things," he said. "For the longest time I wondered why They didn't just end it all and start over again fresh. This world seems such a lost cause, I didn't think we deserved another chance. It came to me, after awhile, how different Their outlook must be, and as I thought about it I got the perspective you need sometimes.

153

Theirs is greatness, but by its magnitude it must be so provincial. Who was Leonardo, next to a tree, or Tolstoy next to a tidal pool? What's Rome, compared to a star?

"In the end I realized that even so, we must be worthiest of all, to hold our own when judged against such perfection. Why else would They bother? But now, They know the time's almost here for Them to interfere with us more directly, even though They know that holds its own peril. They're shaking the dice of the universe."

"What must the Messiah do?" I asked.

"Think with Their mind, and see with our eyes. Then everyone involved can understand."

"There couldn't have been any other way to do this?"

"Why is the sky blue and not green?" he asked. "I don't know, Joanna. I guess not. Sometimes you know, you don't know, you understand, you can't understand—"

"There's too much now that I know without understanding yet," I said. "This way and no other?"

"I have to be truthful," he said. "I'd've preferred another way, myself."

"I love you, Lester," I said, not expecting a response; no longer wishing for one, certainly not hoping for one. He nodded. "Why must it be so unavoidable?"

"Cain and Abel," he said. "Jesus and Judas, Kennedy and Oswald, Nazis and Jews. God and Godness. Without the dark, would the light seem half as bright?"

TEN

• • •

"**D**id he elaborate this morning?" I asked Lester as we rode through the Bronx, passing the abandoned stadium, driving through the Army-guarded courthouse district. The street was blocked on our left, where a building's facade, feeling the tug of years, slumped onto the pavement to take its rest. We sat in the back of the car; Avi sat up front, considering all we cruised by, seeming deaf to our worlds. "I hardly saw him. What did he have to say?"

"Not a lot," Lester said. "He thanked me again. I don't think it was for helping Mrs. Dryden. It was like he was thanking me in advance for what he thinks I'll do. I tried to remind him that I had no say in the matter, but all he did was smile and nod his head."

"Once he conceives his reality everyone's stuck with it," I said.

155

"You see Mrs. Dryden before she left?" he asked.

"She avoided me. Didn't look very pleased about anything, but then she never does. She didn't even look at her newspaper."

"Has she already taken off?"

"Her flight wasn't leaving until late this afternoon."

"You think this's been his plan all along?" Lester asked. "What he wants me to do?"

"It'd be so unlike him to have a specific goal in mind," I said. "Do you think They'll have a response to his request?"

"They'll answer, but I don't know how."

"Would They involve Themselves if They didn't have to?"

"I've never understood Their criteria," he said. "Why They send church buses off roads into rivers. Why steeples blow down in windstorms. Why so many saints died young. Maybe They would. Maybe not."

The streets around us appeared not to have been swept for years; where windows weren't boarded over, or shuttered closed, they had been broken out, leaving over the sidewalks an icy frosting of bright broken crystal, a diamond-paved road. As Brooklyn and Queens were now part of the no-man's land across the river, and as Staten Island had seceded years before, the Bronx remained the only borough other than Manhattan still existing under the nominal aegis of the government of the City of New York; yet, the Bronx was to Manhattan as a colony might stand in relation to its ruling empire: a strategic outpost whose inhabitants could be easily overlooked, whose defenses required constant supervision.

"There'd be any number of things They could do, I suppose—"

"Limitless," he said. "Godness would leave the details to God. That's where His interest lies, after all."

My father's family were from the Bronx; it was so hard to imagine anyone living here. My grandparents lived near the

Hub, at 149th and Third, until they moved to Co-Op City. The rot they'd escaped trailed them, but didn't catch up until they were long gone. What had been the South Bronx was now nothing other than sweeping acres of brick left to erode back into the earth from which they had been taken, a postindustrial compost heap. In the north Bronx, and along the border, the neighborhoods were indistinguishable from those of southern Westchester, far from Thatcher's estate: that is to say, decrepit, overcrowded, dangerous and awaiting a perpetually delayed rediscovery. Army personnel were stationed throughout the Bronx, for no reasons other than to secure the southeast quadrant against assault from Long Island, and to protect the homes in Riverdale which so many officers had commandeered for themselves. The population had proved so efficient at killing itself off that assistance from the Army was seen as unnecessary; the average Bronxite's life, in those days, was twenty-three. Jensen, a newer immigrant, entered half-life at twenty-seven.

"Where is everybody?" Lester asked, seeing along the Concourse nothing but endless blocks of emptied buildings. I shook my head. Signs were posted upon rusted window-grates and locked doors, familiar signs seen throughout the borough, each of standard design, each bearing the yellow grin and pro forma notification: PROPERTY OF DRYCO. NO TRESPASSING. "I wouldn't think he'd find this neighborhood a sound investment."

The farther north we drove, the more people we saw; one or two per block. "He has plans," I said. "He started buying it up several months ago. You know the wall downtown, around the Battery?" Lester nodded. "He foresees the water rising high enough one day to warrant moving the operations up here, Bernard tells me. He'll tear it all down eventually. I hesitate to think what he'll build in its place—"

"Did he make everyone leave?"

"Not everyone," I said. More natives came into view: remaining residents huddled at street-corners, leaned against doorways, clung to lampposts as if expecting the wind to rise and carry them all away. They seemed only partially real, as if the uncertain conditions under which they lived caused them, over time, to fade away before they might be erased. In the lot of an abandoned gas station a cluster of thin women watched two older men circle around each other, lifting their arms over their heads, performing some manner of ghost dance upon the asphalt plain.

"Thatcher believes you can bring Jensen out of his coma, I'm sure," I said.

"I'd think that if he came out of it Thatcher'd only kill him when he was done with him. I doubt he'd want to be reawakened, considering."

We turned onto Gun Hill Road; in those days, an appropriate name. The hospital buildings rose before us, appearing as an embassy in a war-torn country. Surrounding streets were secured by countless guards; atop stacks of sandbags were head-high coils of razor-edged wire. Our driver edged us past concrete pyramids and stelae erupting at unpredictable intervals through the road's pavement. At several checkpoints we were allowed passage, and moved to the next station. Through our car's insulating walls I grew conscious of a distant whirring, the sound of a swarm of locusts.

"Where are we going in?" I asked.

"The emergency room entrance is safest," Avi said, speaking to us through the intercom. "We had no information at the office as to how we reach the experimental floor—"

"I thought we ran it."

"That doesn't mean we know anything about it. We'll ask at the desk once we're inside."

Looking out the window as we rounded one last corner, I saw the source of the oncoming noise. A covey of Emergency

Medical and police helicopters was settling down across the way in a vacant field smoothed down by repeated landings. The breeze whipped up by the rotors lifted the dry soil toward heaven, spinning it into dust devils.

"Stick close," Avi said as we got out of the car, walking swiftly into the hospital and passing through the emergency room's electronically locked bars. The Bronx's missing population rose up around us: hundreds were jammed into the waiting room, crammed in shoulder-to-shoulder along benches attached to the walls, lying in heaps, on stretchers or on blankets aligned in haphazard rows upon the floor. Children's high crescendoes rose in atonal counterpoint against adults' hushed drones. Hospital staff stepped warily through the crowds as if over a minefield, handing out forms, taking temperatures with digital thermometers, giving small cups of water to the overheated, slipping drugs to those who'd come ready to bribe. Nine television sets, none working, hung from the ceiling, attached to a grotesque chandelier; their pulsing screens sedated and soothed those awaiting who chose to look up.

Avi tugged at an extern's sleeve; the man coughed, sounding tubercular.

"How do we get to the experimental floor?"

"No English," he said, in that language. The first patients from the helicopters began coming in. We stepped aside, allowing the newcomers entry.

"Out of the way," an orderly screamed, pushing a gurney stacked three deep across the floor. "Nurse! Get 'em ready back there."

"Yo, yo, watch your back, watch your back—"

"Nurse!"

An unending stream of gurneys carried in the casualties: young blacks, Latinos, and police, men and women—that is, those old enough to be called men and women. Those police still on active service assisted in clearing the way for their own, kicking aside people lying on the floor that the space they occupied might be used. They swung their clubs with impunity, surely estimating that it was safe to do so while medical personnel were so near.

"Avi, get us out of here," I said. "This is dangerous—"

"Legal danger, though," he said. "Stay with me."

A supervising nurse greeted one of the police captains; together they judged their patients. Orderlies hustled away each gurney bearing a policeperson, once the captain ascertained their condition; civilians weren't sped off with such fervor. The nurse paused at each to await the captain's word before marking, or not marking, upon each patient's forehead the mark of solace, the purple X of triage. A young man whose legs were gone below the knees wailed so loudly as to drown out all others' screams. The captain patted his head.

"Keep this one," he said to the nurse; the youth was moved along. A woman lay on the next gurney, her ankles cuffed to the metal bars supporting the mattress; her hands were tied above her head.

"What about her?" the nurse asked. It was impossible to guess what the woman could have done, and the captain didn't say; before I could turn away he shot her in the head. Those in the room who were able, or whose television-induced trance was not too deep, threw themselves to the floor. I held Lester tightly as we followed Avi to the admittance desk.

"You saw that," I said. "You saw it." Lester had no reply; what could he add? The captain and the nurse continued on their rounds.

"Excuse me," Avi said, shouting through the protective mesh running from desktop to ceiling. No one looked up. "How do we get to the experimental floor?"

"Take a number," a nurse shouted back, gesturing to a machine bolted onto the desktop, one of those devices delis once used to keep their customers under control.

"Where's the elevator to the experimental floor?"

"There's no experimental floor."

"How do we get to it?"

"Lester," I said, unable to forget the woman's face as she lay there; I wouldn't have said she appeared surprised. "Can't something be done to help? This is unbearable—"

"In these situations it isn't right to help one without helping all," he said. "It'd hardly be possible—"

"Why?"

"It'd be like sending a hundred times the normal current through a kitchen appliance. There's no getting around it. I'm sorry, Joanna, the spirit is willing but the flesh is weak."

"If there were an experimental floor," Avi said to a different nurse as she emerged from behind a row of dented filing cabinets, "how would you get to it?"

"Down that hall, fifth elevator on the right," she said, pointing. Avi smiled, and wrapped his arms around us; we walked toward the hall. The captain and the nurse were ahead of us; that woman's face could have been pressed against mine, so clear was her memory. My brain felt aflame; the captain's knees buckled, as if he were dizzy, overcome by what he had done. There was no guilt in his soul. The nurse grabbed him as he fell.

"Joanna," Lester said, shaking me. "No."

The captain stood without moving for a moment; shook his head, and continued on. We edged past them, and counted off the elevators until we found the fifth one. As its doors slid apart, revealing within walls so white as snow, I found myself wondering if we'd found the way by which we could go much further than we could have ever hoped, or feared. "What's wrong, Joanna?" Avi asked.

"This is such an awful place," I said. "It brings out the worst in everyone, I suppose—"

"People wouldn't get sick unless they brought it on themselves—"

"Avi, shut up." We ascended; I looked to Lester, who stood close by me, patently aware of what I'd felt, and continued to feel. "There was no reason for what he did—"

"The captain?" Avi asked. "In his mind there must have been. People lose their patience sometimes, that's all."

"Even divine retribution is less than divine," said Lester, touching my hand. "Don't forget that."

"We have to take precautions," Avi said, removing his wallet from his pocket, holding it open before him that his Dryco ID might be immediately visible. "Stay behind me, in the corners. Make sure you can be seen. Hold your arms in front of you, palms out."

The elevator stopped, the door opened; Avi yelled "Dryco!" and thrust his wallet forward as if it might defend. A large man in a blue uniform balanced what appeared to be a cannon against his paunch, leveling the weapon at Avi's midriff. A younger man in a suit stepped up, plucking the wallet from Avi's hand, smiling as if he'd happened upon autumn's last perfect apple, still hanging from its tree.

"Easy," he said to the armed man, and, still smiling, handed Avi's wallet back to him. "Trust good, control better. Accompanied?"

"Obviously," said Avi, guiding us out into the entrance hall. I looked more closely at the guard's gun, knowing nothing of artillery than what I'd seen at play. It resembled half a dozen shotguns bundled together and tied with two handgrips. "In a hospital you're using this sort of thing?"

"Fireplus," said the overseer. "Ready to reprise."

"We're here to see Jensen," Avi said. "He's a persistent vegetable. Arrangements were made. Which is his room and where is it?"

"328," the man said, taking badges that bore our logo upon a forest-green field from his pocket, handing them to us. "Thirty top permissible with PVs. Don't overstimulate."

"Unintended," said Avi, pinning his insignia to his lapel. The man pressed a button, and a buzzer rang; a steel door disappeared into a slot in the ceiling. The walls of the long hall beyond were painted sky blue; soft-edged patches of white dotting the azure represented clouds, so near as I could tell.

"What did you mean, persistent vegetable?" I asked.

"Referring to his state," Avi said. "They're exact in their terminology around here. It's good to go along."

"What sort of gun was that?" Lester asked.

"A topbreak," said Avi. "Six 20-gauge magnum barrels fixed and mounted, revolving and firing hollowpoints in sequence. A tube in the center squirts hydrochloric acid."

"Since when do you know from guns?" I asked.

"You learn." A flock of doctors flew down the hall, giving no evidence that they considered us worthy of study. Their long white coats billowed as clumsy wings behind them. As we moved through the hall's bends and turns we began coming upon doors left partially open, or completely ajar; each room held no more than two patients, fast in their beds, nursed by machinery. Some were hooked up to dialysis units; others slept beneath translucent tents.

"What sort of experiments go on on an experimental floor?" Lester asked.

"Ask the experimenters," said Avi. "This looks like the place. 328, wasn't it?" This door was shut; he rapped once against its wood, and then again.

"Is it locked?"

"Would it matter?" Turning the knob we opened the door. The windowless room was soaked in unshadowed fluorescence; one unknowing might have thought medical science knew no higher aim than to preserve the tans of those convalescing. Jensen lay naked on his back atop a heated mattress. Three machines attended to his needs; wires ran from their mantles and attached to clamps on his forehead, arms, and legs. From his scattered parts tubes drained into bottles, bags, and jars. In the screens of his caretakers I discerned nothing but glowing lines and phosphorescent flashes. He had an erection; I wondered briefly whether his condition produced it or if it was induced, and then I noted the bend of his catheter, curving up and then down again, appearing after a time no more remarkable than a bishop's crook.

"Did you know him?" Avi asked.

"No," I said. "He's so young. They hire them so young nowdays."

"They're more impressionable, fresh from college."

The muscle with which Jensen's body was padded assured me that he'd never done a day's worth of physical labor in his life; his flesh could have been hardened foam, shaped to suit. I'd known several co-workers who'd suffered coronaries while applying bulk suitable enough to convince supervisors that they could handle the strain of an executive career. "I guess it's up to you at this point," Avi said.

"Lester?" I asked. Until that moment he'd waited at the room's threshold, as if approaching too quickly without suitable preparation might disturb whatever mood needed first to be set. Walking to the bedside he pressed his fingertips against Jensen's forehead, careful not to dislodge the wires. Jensen's eyes were open, but he couldn't see; the pupils were so small as to be absent. As Lester made contact we listened to the machines' vespers: beeps, pings, brief gasps of static, and a soft choral hum.

"Any luck?" I asked. Lester suddenly drew his hand up, as if in probing for something dropped he'd jammed his fingers into a wall socket.

"What was it?" Avi asked. "What? What'd you see—?"

"Who're you?" A stranger's voice, coming so unexpectedly that, before we turned to see who it might be, I considered that perhaps Jensen was awake after all, employing ventriloquism to make us go away. "You going to answer?" the woman asked; she was tall and wore a candy-striped uniform. Her hair was set in cornrows; her forearms were more muscular than Jensen's. "You family or what?"

"We're with Dryco," Avi said. "So was he. We came to visit."

"Everybody on this floor's with Dryco, hear them tell it. You all may own the place but that doesn't mean you can run around here like you were home."

"We intended no trouble—"

"None of you all never do. You know how easy it is to spread diseases to somebody in his shape? You come in with the sniffles and it'll be pneumonia once he gets it. Who you think'll have to deal with the mess?"

"I'm sorry," I said. "We'll leave—"

"Not so fast. I'm saying be careful. Long as you're here, one of you give me a hand flipping him."

"Why does he need flipping?" Avi asked.

"Even on these special mattresses they get bedsores if you don't watch 'em. Let 'em lie too long in one place, they draw all in on themselves. Wind up looking like a pretzel. Then you got to break their damn arms and legs to straighten 'em out again. So, you got to turn 'em, once, twice a day." She regarded her patient. "Somebody's glad to see me this morning," she said, yanking the catheter free, and then unclipping the other wires, and tubes.

"Are you the floor nurse?" I asked, reading the name on her badge so that I could call her by her name, and so not treat her only as a creation of the hospital. "Nurse Cordero?"

"I'm paramed." She detached the last connections and removed the intravenous tube from his left arm's vein. "I'll get his legs, you put your hands under him. When I say go, turn him over on his right side. Okay?"

"All right—" said Avi.

"Do you attend him every day?" I asked.

"Doctors attend, I just clean up after 'em. This's the only chance I get to relax, making the rounds up here."

"Has he ever shown signs of consciousness?"

"No. Stiff as a board. He'll blink his eyes sometimes if the lights dim but that's involuntary, you know these PVs. Ready now? Get your hands under there. Don't want to bruise anything useful. Okay, go."

They folded him as if he were an omelet. Lester had said nothing since removing his hands from Jensen's head. He'd picked something up, I knew, and had returned to his place by the door. Nurse Cordero began reinserting the tubes and reclamping the wires.

"A week or so ago I had a day off," she said. "Not long after they brought him in. Girl who's on duty when I'm not told me he started mumbling about something—"

"Did she say what?"

"Nothing she could understand," she said, wielding the catheter so deftly that she could have been threading a needle. "She told the doctor in charge that she thought he might be coming out of it. Told me he got on the phone to somebody real worried like before she even got out of his office. But when I came in, next morning, he looked just the same to me."

"Which doctor was that?"

"Whichever one was in charge, I don't remember. Around here one's as good or bad as the next."

After hooking up one final cord she paused, and wiped the perspiration from her forehead with the side of her hand. "Well, I'd think he's had about as much visiting'll be good for him. Never can tell how the outside's affecting the inside."

"What do you mean?" I asked.

"Got to keep him fresh. You know."

"Fresh for what?" Avi asked.

"Recycling."

"What are you talking about?" I asked. "Recycling what?"

"What he's got," she said. "You said you're with the

166

company, you ought to know. Word passed along this morning gave the okay. Next week, he's part and parceled."

She nodded that we should follow her as she left the room. "Maybe you all don't understand how it works up here," she said. "Some of the folks up here, are best kept like they are. Others, though, there's not that much they can find out from 'em no matter how long they're around, and there's new ones coming in all the time. Only so much space up here."

"What are you getting at?" Avi asked.

"When they're young and healthy like he is, and have no relatives, and once we flush the poisons or the drugs out of their systems, well, they cut off the machines and then—"

"Distribute the parts to worthy recipients," I said.

"Within the company, as I understand it," she said. "Cost-effective, I imagine."

"Then he's to be put up for auction?" Avi asked.

"First come, first served, long as you can afford it," she said. "That's why I was so rough on you at first, didn't know what you were fiddling with. He's in perfect shape at the moment."

"And you wanted to keep him that way," I said.

"You understand," she said, and looked him over as he lay there. "They always take the best-looking ones."

After she let us out, closing the door behind us, we stood in the hall for several moments, saying nothing.

"Come along to his apartment with me," Avi said. "Let's see what we find over there."

"How long has Dryco owned the building?" I asked as we stepped from the car onto the Grand Concourse at 167th Street. We crossed the broad sidewalk to the building's entrance, crushing beneath our feet glass vials as empty as the boulevard.

"Over a year," Avi said. "It belonged to one of the realty companies he obtained." With little effort he forced open the building's broken door. "Jensen moved in when his grandmother died. I think he was the only one still living here. Dryco kept the utilities running."

The lobby was only large enough to be called unassuming. Ocher paint peeled away from the lower reaches of the walls; above that watermark were graffiti surely scrawled on while I was still at college. In making our way to his apartment we passed the elevators; none was working. Someone had pried the doors from their frames and left them lying on the cold, stained tile.

"This one's his," Avi said, drawing from his jacket a bracelet ringed with keys, and beginning to unlock the door's seven locks. Jensen's flat was in the rear of the building, on the ground floor; I gathered that it faced the smaller street running just to the east of the Concourse.

"They never let on they'd be putting him up for sale," I said, attempting to judge Avi's reaction, to see if he'd already known.

"It's understandable," he said.

"And convenient," I said. "Did Bernard have anything particularly in mind that you should be looking for?" I leaned against the wall, having certified beforehand that no roaches scurried nearby that could take advantage of my proximity. There *were* no roaches, which was something other than unusual.

"Evidence," said Avi, shoving his way in. As we entered I knew a sudden notion that I'd been there before; remembered visiting, as a child, an elderly aunt who lived on the Concourse some twenty blocks to the north. Her apartment had been no different from Jensen's, speaking only of layout: within was a small foyer, a kitchen and bath, two bedrooms and a living room sunk two steps below the level of the other rooms.

"Do you think he was here much?" Avi asked, looking around.

"Why do you ask?" At once I realized why, when my eyes

adjusted to the dim. Brown curtains hid casement windows, dyeing all in sepia. If the Metropolitan Museum's curators ever chose to admit into its collection of period rooms one representing the Eisenhower era, they could never have found one more perfect than Jensen's; his grandmother's, I should say. An armless sofa stretched along the right side of the living room, its boomerang-shaped legs lifting its sections no more than a foot from the floor; the drawers of a Danish Modern cabinet bore no matching blond-wood handles, none that were visible. A floor-to-ceiling pole lamp appeared braced in such a way as to support the ceiling; what appeared as an artist's oversized palette bore stubby legs, that it might be used as a table. A wall clock resembled a splattered melon thrown against the plaster-work. Black aluminum bookcases contained scores of old paperbacks; along their top shelves were photographs in faux-brass frames.

"No disputing taste," said Avi. A film of dust coated everything, as if it had been applied in careful layers to serve as protection. Walking across the room to one of the bookcases, coughing as I drew in breaths thick with unsettled dust, I took from the shelves several volumes. *Pride and Prejudice*'s cover showed a busty Regency wench wielding a whip, and I hesitated to imagine the workings of the art director's mind. When I opened *The Flying Saucers Are Real*, the cover's cellophane epidermis scaled loose beneath my fingers, and the pages crumbled into flakes of brown snow.

"Who's pictured?" Avi asked, coming over, puffs of dust rising with his every footstep. Within moments we were all coughing.

"It must be his family. Her family. He's in this one—"

"The kid?"

"Look at the ears. That's him."

There were no other shots of Jensen; in this single image he sat on the lap of an older woman; she sat on the living room's sofa. He looked too young for elementary school.

She wore a simple flowered frock; one arm was thrown over him, to keep him from sliding away. At first I thought she hadn't washed before having her picture taken. "Must be his grandmother," Avi said.

"What's that on her arm?" As I stared into the photo, attempting to raise its image into life, I found myself unable to distinguish smudge from shadow.

"Numbers," Avi said. Looking again, I saw them.

"They didn't do that everywhere, did they?" I asked. "Maybe she even knew your father—"

"No."

The other, older photographs were taken a world away, and preserved seconds of years long lost. Though I was no photographer I knew at once that their earthen tones had been weathered in, and not painted on. In the largest shot, a man with mustache, bowler, and boutonniere stood with a woman wearing a cloche, and a long coat; judging from her waist I imagined she'd had several children. They'd been captured in the midst of a square cobbled over with stones no larger than a young girl's breast; piercing the sky behind their heads were ornate spires, eight-gabled roofs, filigreed stone and the statue of an angel hewn into a facade.

"I think that's Prague," I said.

"They'd have been hidden somewhere," Avi said.

"The pictures?" I asked, looking over the rest; there were twenty-odd photos, and different people in each. Only the shot of Jensen and his grandmother appeared to have been taken in America.

"Buried, maybe. Stuffed behind bricks in a chimney. That's how my father saved a couple of things."

"And come back for them later."

"If they could." Avi sighed, and turned away. "I'll be quick," he said. "I feel like a thief."

He walked up the two steps and disappeared behind the bedroom doors. Lester sat on the edge of the sofa; I sat down beside him. The yellow-brown light strained through the curtains made the room seem sealed within amber.

"What's in his head?" I asked.

"It's easier to say what isn't there," said Lester.

"Say it, then."

"Nothing involving Japan, or that fellow Otsuka. Nothing about Gus, except an impression of surprise. Nothing about his family or anyone who might once have been close to him. He did want to tell Thatcher something. I couldn't tell what, exactly. Something he saw. There was a hatred there that didn't leave room for much else. That sort of thing tends to linger."

"Hatred toward whom?"

"A general rage," he said. "Toward Bernard, to some degree."

"What was it that he saw?" I asked; Lester sat within a faint cloud, seeming to stir up dust by the act of remembering. "You acted like you were burned when you were in there."

"Some memories hurt more than others."

"Did you see what he saw?"

The rumble of a truck, or of some heavy vehicle, pulling up and coming to a stop sounded through the window, seeming some distance away. Doors slammed as its riders climbed out.

"I saw what remained," Lester said. "I gathered it was a recent memory, it lay too close to the surface, probably he'd been trying to dig a hole for it, and hadn't dug deep enough. He stood on a dock, or a pier. There was water, and boats. He looked down on a boat. Someone lifted a hatch cover—" He paused.

"What else?" I asked. "Lester, tell me—"

"In dredging another's memories you haul up a lot of mud," he said. "There was a disconnection, and then another picture. There were people. They seemed to be

171

dead. Then I think he must have changed the channel, as it were."

Whoever had parked outside wasn't coming in, I didn't believe, or they would have already broken in the door the rest of the way; I heard truck doors open once more, and murmurs of conversation too distant to make out. Children were laughing, as if leaving school.

"This has something to do with all of this?"

"Without question."

"Was there anything else?"

"The soul remains trapped for only so long," Lester said. "Afterward, it's like digging up a bone and then trying to imagine its animal."

Bile rose from my belly up my throat as I heard a crash in the other room; leaping up, I realized it was only Avi, emptying drawers that he might rifle Jensen's more disposable fragments. Lester sat as before, moving no muscles but those that allowed him breath. At that moment he looked as beyond any attentions I might offer as had Jensen. A child shouted, out on the street; I walked over to the window, curious to see. Spiders dropped onto my fingers as I drew back the musty curtains and pulled apart the dust-blackened blinds. A white van bearing on its side a red cross made a U-turn in the middle of the back street. No one who might have made noise was visible. As the van drove away, heading southeast, I eyed the cross more closely; where red nave met red transept a small yellow circle fit neatly into the interstice.

"Lester?" I asked; he didn't answer. "What's wrong?"

"It's the time," he said. "Nothing more. Is Avi all right? He looked so uncomfortable when you mentioned his father."

"They're just like this," I said, holding up two fingers in a sign of victory, or of peace. "They're from different worlds, that's all."

"His father was in a concentration camp?"

172

"His father," I said, "and his father's first wife, and their children and families. He married Avi's mother after the war. He told me they met in a displaced persons' zone—"

"Most people do, I suppose," he said. Avi stepped out of the bedroom just then, his hands smeared with dust and dirt. He held several sheets of paper, folded in such a way as to hide the writing. When he looked at us he appeared oddly calm, for the first time since we'd encountered Lester: as if, having been at first frightened by a shape in his room at night, and unable to cry for his mother, he'd strengthened his will enough that he might look more closely and, having allowed his eyes to readjust to the dark, saw at second glance that the shape was nothing that could bear harm; found at last, upon rising, that his terror came solely from misperception, a trick played on the eye by his soul.

"What were you talking about?" he asked.

"Your father," Lester said; For an instant Avi appeared as if upon rising he'd discovered that sometimes something does lurk in rooms at night. When he recovered he proceeded as if he'd been told nothing more than the time.

"What happened to him, you mean?" Avi asked. "He lived."

"Where was he?"

"They put him in Auschwitz first," Avi said. "Then he was sent to Maidanek."

"And then?"

Avi said nothing for a moment; stared at the papers in his hand. "There's no purpose in the telling."

"There was a purpose in its occurring," said Lester.

"The Allies were closing in," Avi said, his face holding no expression, his voice carrying no inflection as he told Lester; once he'd told me, using similar phrasing, and like tone, and I could only think that he recounted it as he'd heard his father tell it to him. "The Germans moved a thousand prisoners from Maidanek, deeper into Germany. The prisoners were all men and my father was one of them.

They reached a small town on a cloudless day. The soldiers had orders to get rid of the prisoners. They locked them in a big brick barn and set fire to it. The prisoners screamed. My father said they screamed so loud that finally even God heard their prayers. It rained. The fire went out. Most of them were already dead. My father, a few others, they lived."

He had nothing more to add, not immediately; we sat in the room, watching the light fade around us as the afternoon drew to a close. After a short time more Avi spoke again, directing his words toward Lester, as if I wasn't even there. "I know there must be a purpose to everything," he said. "But where's the purpose in that?"

"Would you be standing here telling the story to me if there'd been no purpose?" Lester asked.

"Where's the purpose?" Avi repeated. "What was God's intent? Can you say?"

"Only God could say," Lester said. "Godness draws what good She can from evil. So Her tears saved enough for a minyan."

Avi closed his eyes; forgetting for the moment what he was, he seemed to remember, for an instant, what he had been. Lester crossed the room, that he could stand beside him.

"Do what you must," he said. "It's your job, Avi. You know that."

Avi opened his eyes, and nodded his head; started to close his hand, as if to crumple the papers he held. When he saw Lester demurring he stopped, and folded them over one more time, and slipped them into his jacket.

"Lester," I said, "What is it?" I don't know why I asked; I knew.

"Mister Dryden will have to see these, Joanna," Avi said, patting his pocket. "He has to. I'm sorry. Lester's right."

I followed them out of the apartment, down the hall, and into the street. Avi held Lester close to him as he guided him into the car, into the back seat; for the only time during the years I worked for Dryco I sat up front where the guards always sat, protecting us without cease until the time came to take us away. I wanted to hold Lester; feared I would never recall the feel of his touch, years later, though I knew it was foolish of me to have such fears. The sunset was so beautiful that it hurt to see. God favors details, truly; Godness appears only in absences, and I saw no sign of rain.

ELEVEN

• • • • • • •

Three hours later Jake and Bernard hustled me into the car; Thatcher was already inside. When we went back to Dryco I'd been locked in my office, as if I'd try to get away. Thatcher had come in to sit with me awhile; after so long he departed, leaving neither explanation nor conclusion behind.

"What are you doing to him? Where is he?"

"You've got to let us handle this, hon," Thatcher said. "You're taking this more seriously than you ought to—"

"I don't want to hear it," I said. "What were those papers Avi had? Will you please tell me something other than lies?"

"What else can we offer, sweetness?" said Bernard. "I prefer to give you truth if you seem capable of dealing with it. You know that."

"The papers show Lester was approached by Otsuka's boys earlier this year," Thatcher said, staring through the windshield at the narrow street before us. "He's admitted it. Told us it went no further than that. We have no reason to think otherwise. Said he didn't even realize until the other day that they might even have been connected to Otsuka. Says the ones who did the contacting weren't Japanese. It's not a pretty tale."

"It appears Otsuka heard the same stories as we did," said Bernard, "and proposed similar options through his agents. He simply didn't woo with such intensity as did we, and certainly he hadn't such good bait. Call it a hunch, but I doubt that theology played much of a part in their actions. I'd think driving messianic delusions into Shintoism could prove problematic."

"I still think it's funny none of the Europeans got into the act—" said Thatcher.

"They probably tried," said Bernard. "When all these lovers come calling, what's a boy to do?"

"If he had nothing to do with them what difference does it make?" I asked. "Why are you doing this?"

"He could have gone along," said Thatcher, by way of explanation. "He just didn't. But he could have."

"Macaffrey is rather too intent on keeping secrets," said Bernard. "Not necessarily a useful trait if he's to attain the sort of position some around here would have him attain. It's a matter he should have found appropriate at some time to mention to us, and he didn't. He said nothing to you, I'm sure—"

"This is insane," I said. "Nobody keeps more secrets than you two."

"A number of which he's discovered since signing on with us. And he is uncannily adept at making inferences regarding situations best left alone. There's no way around it, Joanna, the teacher needs a lesson of his own."

"Even a messiah can't think he can get away with anything he wants to do," said Thatcher. "We hear anything from Susie yet? Shouldn't she be there by now?"

"She's only just landing, Thatcher. Give it until nine or nine-thirty. Let her get there, why don't you?"

"I just asked—"

"What are you doing to Lester?" I repeated. "Where is he?"

"Please calm down, hon," Thatcher said. "We're going to see him now. We had him taken over to the Tombs. They got some new techniques in development over there Bernard thought could be productively applied. I gave the go-ahead."

"You're going to torture him," I said.

"What kind of people you think we are?" Thatcher asked. "We won't do anything to him that'll hurt him physically."

"Think of it as motivational training," said Bernard. "Some call it neopavlovianism. We leave him with a few lasting impressions. Nothing new. Simply reenforcing what's already there, in the event he chooses to stray."

"But what is it?"

"Elegant," he continued. "We recreate for the subject a key event in the subject's life."

"What sort of event?"

"Ideally, a childhood trauma. They can come in so handy later on, if put to worthy purpose. The doctors believe this treatment will be helpful not only for us but for the subject as well—"

"Lester," I said, interrupting. "Not subject. Lester."

"You say tomato," said Bernard. "In any event, by enabling him to reexperience a chosen trauma, lifting it to the surface of his mind, he has a second chance to deal with its effects, using knowledge since gained and—oh, how do they put it?—life experiences to get a better grasp on the inescapable. Everyone's better off afterward, possibly."

* * *

The Tombs was in the Criminal Courts Building, on Centre Street, not far from Dryco headquarters. Years ago criminals awaiting trial were held in cells on the upper floors; when the new jail was built to the north of the older structure, those upper floors were renovated for new uses, through a joint effort of the city government and Dryco.

"Behavioral science is such a growth industry," Bernard continued. "I'm told this particular technique is especially useful conjoined with traditional psychiatric approaches, though I don't have to tell you about my qualms concerning psychiatry. The only Freud I appreciate is schadenfreude. Still, now that something more scientific has been added to the mix—"

"What have you done to him so far?"

"A brief isolation," Bernard said. "He was given a light sedative, to assist in calming him before the next step, a little walk down memory lane."

Our car pulled into the garage that had been built below the new jail. The elevators that rose through the old building, leading to the Tombs, could be reached through a series of secured tunnels that ran under the street beneath the structures.

"You ever been here before, hon?" Thatcher asked.

"For jury duty," I said. "Six years ago."

"It's a fascinating place, whatever you've heard. You know how shaggy dog stories shed."

"The new computer's mainframe will be installed here directly above the interrogation floor," said Bernard. "It's a good central location."

The elevator reserved for Dryco's use took us up; when we emerged we entered a hall that appeared so washed of personality that it could have been any office building. Discarded monitors, keyboards, and desks were piled high along the walls; the lights flickered and hissed, and smelled of burning tar. Police and men in cheap suits went about their business until they saw Thatcher approaching; then they'd flatten themselves against uncluttered walls until we passed, Bernard and I coming directly behind him, Jake bringing up the rear. We reached what appeared to be the end of the hall. Bernard, stepping forward, pressed a light switch; the wall blocking our progress slid out of sight, revealing a shorter hall beyond, and two unmarked doors.

"That one leads to the staging area," said Bernard, nodding to the door on the left, opening the one on the right. "The observation room. Let us observe."

"Stay back here, Jake," Thatcher said, and Jake took his place by the door once we entered. Walking in, we saw ourselves walking toward us. A mirror: one as high and wide as the room, serving as barrier between staging area and observatory. An oak table was placed perpendicular to the mirror, and the table's chairs were turned away from the door. Two men wearing long white coats were already in the room; I gathered that they could be called doctors. They shifted in their chairs and greeted us.

"Hello, Frank," Bernard said, shaking hands with the older of the pair, a man in his late fifties with a red, wattled neck. His cheeks were scarred with pockmarks; his white hair retained enough blond to lend his crown a greenish corrosion. "How's he holding up? All progressing?"

"His injection was administered twenty minutes ago," Frank said. "Optimum timeframe begins shortly and lasts for an hour and a half."

"Shouldn't think it'd take that long," said Thatcher, pulling out a chair for me that I might have a seat. "This is Joanna, folks."

"He mentioned you," said Frank. "You've made an impression on an impressionable mind."

"She has that tendency," said Bernard.

"What are you shooting him up with?" I asked.

"Let's let these old junkies explain. Medical terminology so disturbs my ears. Howard?"

"The patient receives 450 cc's of Pentathline blended

with a trace of Metalysergic," Howard, the younger doctor, replied. Something about him reminded me of the boys I knew in high school biology class, the ones who liked to help the teachers pass out the new-pithed frogs. "Pentathline enables the patient to recall repressed information in infinite detail, while Metalysergic's hallucinogenic properties allow him to believe that events described are events occurring."

"Chemical hypnosis," said Frank. "If you told him a match had been applied to his arm, a blister would be raised on the skin."

"When actual events taken from the patient's life are recounted to him, the combined chemicals produce in the mind an ongoing reality unrelated to actual surroundings."

"Better n' television," said Thatcher.

"And no unwanted side effects are afterward noticed?" Bernard asked.

"None noticed thus far."

"What are you going to make him remember?" I asked.

"Allow him to remember," Bernard said, correcting me. He opened a folder lying atop a small pile stacked upon the table and, pulling from it two Xeroxes of newspaper articles, handed them to me. The clippings were from the Lexington, Kentucky *Herald*, with dates twenty years distant.

DOCTORS THINK MIRACLE CHILD WILL SURVIVE,

and

LESTER TO TESTIFY IN MOTHER'S TRIAL, DA SAYS

"Sending his own mother to the slammer," said Thatcher. "What a world."

"They had to send her someplace . . ." Bernard said.

"Please explain these," I said, letting the copies drop onto the table.

"He didn't even tell you?" Bernard said. "See what we

mean about this fondness for secrecy? I'd almost call it a fetish."

"One day Lester's mother went a little funny in the head," said Thatcher.

"Afterward," said Bernard, "her sense of purpose persuaded her to plead neither guilt nor insanity. She discharged three lawyers before setting her sights low enough. Young Macaffrey was the only witness for the prosecution, and once he recovered the trial began. His testimony was given in closed session, with only the lawyers and judge present. They were considerate enough to take his age into account. She was convicted, and sentenced. She filed no appeal and so went up the river, or wherever it is they go in Kentucky. Six months later a fire of suspicious origin gutted her cell. She was in it, at the time."

"Suspicious?" I said. "How?"

"Only cause of the fire they could come up with was spontaneous human combustion," said Thatcher.

"Not a favorite of coroners," said Bernard. "It was put down as—" He paused; thumbed through the stack until he found the document he sought. "Death by misadventure," he read. "So Macaffrey was put, briefly, in the care of the commonwealth, poor boy. He was given a remarkable number of tests pertaining to intelligence and personality. He had no surviving family and after a time they began shooting him through a series of foster homes, all the while being periodically tested. Emotional fractures were noted early on, along with a keen but unbalanced intellect. He fooled them enough even then that at one point he was given the Rhine test for ESP. Results were inconclusive, which hardly surprises—"

"Seems he got put in homes where the fathers had lots of time on their hands," said Thatcher. "He got beat pretty regularly in one of 'em, sounds like. He seemed pretty content in another, but then the family moved to Houston to look for work and the agencies responsible for his well-being wouldn't let 'em take him along. They put him in a place where, when the father wasn't beating him, he was molesting his daughters. Lester was fifteen by then. Don't know how old the daughters were, or if he knew about it, or did anything if he did know."

"We know he ran away," said Bernard. "Then for four years we have no record as to what he did, or where he was. He came to New York ten years ago, living in perfect obscurity until the yen to fulfill this perceived role of savior of Loisaida came over him. The rest is silence. Frank, recap results of our tests."

"Pervasive disassociation is noted," said Frank. "Perhaps predisposing the subject to schizophrenic disorder over the next few years. Manic-depressive syndrome in the purest manifestation is not found, though he experiences bouts of severe depression interspersed with episodes where the observable messianic complex would appear to be more pronounced. We find unmistakable signs of ethylithic mythomania—"

"Run that by me again," said Thatcher.

"A tendency to identify oneself too closely with historic events," said Frank. "Believing that one's actions effect one's society, now and in the future, even in the past. Bear in mind that in most studies of even the so-called great, psychotic propensities are always noted. We can say—"

"We can say he's not the sort of fellow we'd like to have our daughters bring home," said Bernard.

"You still don't give him enough credit," said Thatcher.

"He's overspent what he had."

"We'll see," said Thatcher. "Can we get on with this? I don't want to miss Susie when she calls."

"Very well." The room darkened; a white light shone through the mirror with the gleam of the sun striking a glacier. The mirror's glass was two-way; the staging area was lit so evenly, and painted so white, that Lester could have been sitting a foot or a mile away, so absent was perspective. He'd drawn his knees tight against his chest, and clasped his hands around his knees. His labored breathing came as roar over the intercom. Avi entered that room, standing in the far left corner, wearing a knee-length coat. Two mannequins were close by; half-mannequins, truly, resembling sewing dummies with unsculpted heads. Their plaster torsos were mounted upon wheeled tripods.

"Having all source material at hand," said Bernard, sitting next to me, picking up a wireless mike, "court transcripts, police reports, photographs of the house and of his family, testimony given and newspaper accounts, we can begin. Keep in mind that a certain role-playing is essential on the part of the interrogator, and unavoidable on the part of the subject."

"Bernard," I said. "This isn't right. You're punishing him. You're not helping him—"

"Punishment is a biblical precept, I believe," he said. "Onward and downward. Miracle boy? You with us?"

Distance notwithstanding, I saw how his eyes were so dilated that all blue was supplanted by black. He looked across his white world, his head wobbling loosely upon his neck, as if, having once been removed, it hadn't been properly reattached.

"How old are you, Lester?"

"Twenty-nine," he said. With one hand he mussed his hair, as if attempting to comb it. "Think so. Don't know."

"We must be as a child to enter the kingdom of heaven," said Bernard. "You're nine years old."

"Nine," Lester repeated. "Nine years old."

"Very good. Do you recognize where you are? Look around you."

"Where am I?" he asked.

"In the living room of your parents' house. You see it? See the fireplace over there? A big, stone wall? Three brass plates hanging over the wooden mantelpiece? The slate hearth and the butter churn? What else do you see?"

"The andirons," Lester said, reading a swatch of white wall. "A little bench. The dog's basket."

"Every family should have a dog," said Bernard. "What's your dog's name, Lester?"

"Snoopy."

"Original," said Bernard. "Considering your father's profession I'd have thought it might be Saint John the Divine—"

"Mister Leibson," Frank said, lowering his voice, shaking his head. "Don't confuse him unless it's necessary."

Bernard cupped his hand over the microphone's tip. "My fault," he whispered. "Lester? Has Snoopy been acting funny this morning? Almost as if he knew something was wrong?"

"Uh-huh."

"Someone else in the house hasn't been themselves lately either, have they? Who's the troublemaker?"

"I'm twenty-nine," Lester said.

"You're nine years old, Lester. You know what today's date is?"

"No."

"September the nineteenth, 1978. Who's the trouble-maker, Lester?"

Lester drew himself into a ball, and pressed his face against his knees. "Momma."

"Your mother's acting funny? What's she up to?"

"She won't come out of her room," he said. "She won't let Dad in."

"Poor Dad," said Bernard. "Is your sister at home?" Lester nodded once, and stopped. "Her name's Betsy? How old is Betsy? Twelve?" Hearing no answer, Bernard shifted into a new line of questioning. "What's Dad up to right now?"

"He's in the den. Writing his sermon. For tomorrow."

"Today's Saturday, then," Bernard said. "He's listening to music as he writes?"

185

"Yes."

"Reverends should always be reverential of classical music," Bernard said. "What's he listening to? I suspect he's not much for serialism. Nor any heavy romanticism to clog the arteries of the soul."

"Mister Leibson—"

"Choral music is so inspiring." Music rose in volume over unseen loudspeakers, filling both rooms. "Gregorian chants, was it? Bach? Taverner? Our sources aren't so clear on this. Let's say Thomas Tallis. Isn't that lovely music? What do you think of when you hear it?"

"Angels," said Lester. "Millions of angels flying around."

"Worse than gnats, I'd think," said Bernard. "You don't have any trouble seeing the room now, do you?" Lester shook his head; he didn't. "Dog's in his basket. Sis is in her room. Mom's in bed, Dad's communing with spirits. All's right with the world. What are you doing? Were you reading?"

Avi knelt, and slid a book across the floor; it skidded to a stop near Lester's feet. Seeing it, he reached across and picked it up. His hair was wet with perspiration.

"Quite a reader for your age, I hear. What are you reading now?"

"Stories," he said, examining the jacket. "Edgar Allan Poe."

"Good bedtime reading. Isn't that awfully hard reading for a boy your age?"

"I like it," Lester said. "They say it's too hard for me at school. It's not. Dad thinks it's good that I read."

"I suppose your mother has her own opinions."

"She used to think it was good," said Lester. "She says Dad pushes me. Pushes everybody."

"Push comes to shove after so long, doesn't it?"

"They've been fighting a lot lately."

"About what?"

"Everything."

186

"About religion? About God?" Lester nodded. "Didn't they once believe in the same God?"

"Yes."

"Your father's an Episcopal priest?" Lester nodded, again. "Once they believed in a God of love? Now your mother believes in a God of wrath? Well, each to their own. Complicates matters unnecessarily I'd say. What did your father once call your mother, Lester? You know big words, you can say it. What did he call her?"

"Charismatic."

"Sounds like a disease, doesn't it?" said Bernard. "Rather like rabies. God bites the believer and leaves them foaming at the mouth. Dad doesn't think much of this, does he?"

"I hate to hear them fight."

"Do you pray at night for God to make them stop?" Lester nodded his head, and then rested it against his knees again, as if its weight was too great for him to carry unaided. "And God answers some prayers. What's the weather like, by the way?"

"It's been pouring out."

"I gather you mean rain. What they call a frogstrangler in those parts? What time is it now? You see the grandfather clock? By the door to your sister's room. What time is it?"

"Two-thirty."

"Here comes your sister now," Bernard said. "See her?"

"No," said Lester, hiding his face. "Stop it."

Bernard sighed and took a photograph from one of his files; held it before him as he continued. "You see her."

Avi gently pushed one of the mannequins toward Lester; it rolled across the floor on well-oiled wheels, and stopped short of where Lester sat.

"Stop," Lester repeated, still shielding his eyes.

"Don't you love your sister?" Bernard asked. "You haven't seen her in so long. You haven't forgotten what she looks like. Skinny little thing. Taller than you. Straight brown hair and braces. Green eyes. You see her."

Lester cried. "Stop—"

"You're a big boy, Lester. It's all right—"

"Stop it, Bernard," I said. "Look at what you're doing. Stop—"

Thatcher grasped my arm; pulled me nearer. Lester raised his head and looked at the mannequin, smiling through tears. "Bets," he said, and then his smile faded. "Betsy. Talk to me."

"Cat must have her tongue," said Bernard. "She wants to know if you're hungry, Lester. She'll fix you whatever you want to eat. You hungry?" Lester shook his head. "What's she wearing?"

"A white sweater," Lester said. "Blue jeans. Sneakers with pink laces."

Bernard smiled. "Such an eye for detail you've developed. What does she usually fix you to eat on weekends?"

"Grilled cheese sandwiches." The odor of toasting bread permeated the rooms.

"Almost smells good enough to eat, doesn't it? Now you're both in the kitchen, talking about your parents. Isn't the kitchen a homey place? Shame your mother insisted upon painting the walls that dreadful red. Almost like blood, isn't it? You're sitting at that big round table in the center of the room. What communion does your family take there?"

"We have family meetings," Lester said. "Every Wednesday night at seven. After Dad watches the news."

"You discuss family problems at family meetings? Haven't had one for a few weeks, have you?"

"Momma doesn't like to be around us anymore."

"Why's that?"

"She says our sin rubs off on her like dirt."

"Saturday's bath day," said Bernard. "You and your sister hear something. Your father opens the door to his den and comes out. The music's much louder than it was." There came a corresponding increase in volume in our rooms as well; voice upon voice swelled the chorus's sound. "What do you think he's going to do?"

"Try to get Momma to come out."

"What makes you think that?"

"That's what he's always trying to do. She never comes out till she wants to. He's upset. He's yelling at her through the door."

"She probably said something to him. Do you know what? Or why she won't come out?"

Lester got up, and wandered over to the mannequin representing his sister; stroked its unfeatured face. He circled round it, looking her up and down with nothing more than child's intent, seeing so much that he'd lost years before, seeming deaf to our cries.

"Lester," Bernard said, more sharply, holding the microphone so intently that he might have been masturbating. "Tell me why your mother won't come out."

"She thinks we're trying to hurt her."

"Would you hurt your mother?"

Lester made no direct response; he touched the mannequin again and then edged away. "She says we're bad for her soul."

"Does God tell her that?"

"She says Jesus does."

"You Macaffreys are so popular with the Jones Boys," said Bernard. "What does Jesus tell your mother?" Lester shook his head; wouldn't, or couldn't say. "Your parents are yelling at one another through the door? You and Betsy creep over to the kitchen door. You can hear what they're saying but you can't see them."

"Betsy can."

"What is your mother saying to your father?"

"She says Dad blesses too many animals and doesn't think about us."

"Animals?" Bernard asked. "Foxhounds, you mean?"

"No."

"You mean when he blesses the animals in the nativity set at Christmas?" Lester held his hands against his ears as if deafening himself to all he heard. "What animals, Lester? Do you know?"

"People who live in the city," he said. "She says if they were supposed to live at all they wouldn't live like heatherns."

"Did Jesus tell her that? Shame on Jesus. Does your father agree?"

"He says she needs help," Lester said. "Like the people do, but in a different way."

"God helps those who help themselves, I'm told."

"She tells Dad God helps when He wants to."

"She's wise in her generation," said Bernard. "What happens now?"

"She starts screaming. She's not afraid. She's saying curse words. Cursing us."

The smell in the room changed from that of toasting bread to that of burning bread. "What is she screaming about?" Lester sank to his knees upon the white field as if collapsing in the face of a blizzard, knowing it was time to freeze. He wrapped an arm around the mannequin's tripod. I acted without considering; grabbed the microphone from Bernard and shouted into it.

"Lester, don't listen. Don't. Don't listen to it."

Thatcher clamped his hand across my mouth; no sooner did he have me silenced than Bernard wrested the microphone from my hand. It struck me that he seemed willing to break my fingers to retrieve it if he had to. As Thatcher relaxed, somewhat, Bernard picked up, extemporizing.

"Did you hear your sister just then?" Lester lay on the floor, weeping, nodding his head. "She has your best interests at heart. What does your mother say the rest of you want to do with her spirit?"

"Take it to hell," Lester said. "She says we're already burning and we're trying to take her down with us."

"Take her back, I'd say," said Bernard. "Smell something burning, though, don't you? Is it you? No? You two. You forgot all about those sandwiches."

"Bets runs over and takes them off the stove."

"If you'd been paying attention to what needed attention none of this would have happened, would it?" Bernard asked. "But you were too concerned with someone else's business—" I flung out my leg, trying to strike Bernard, but was too far from him to do more than brush his trousers with my shoe.

"Yes—"

"See what happens when you don't give consideration to other people's wishes?" Bernard waited until Lester had stopped wailing, that he might hear his words over the sound of sobs. "You're still having to learn that, aren't you? Well, well. What does your father say now?"

"Nothing."

"Your mother's door opens. You hear it. What does your father say?"

"Put it down," Jake said. "He says put it down."

"Put what down?" Bernard leaned forward, his eyes moist with much that wasn't sad; he breathed through his mouth, as if his excitement so overwhelmed him that he couldn't draw in air enough. "What's the next thing you hear, Lester?"

"Nothing—"

"Your sister saw, Lester. What did she see?"

"I don't know—"

"You do," Bernard said.

"Nothing, nothing, nothing—"

"Tell me—!"

"No!"

The second of the two mannequins was on the far side of the room, near Avi; without words of his own he pulled a shotgun which had been circumcised at each end from beneath his coat and, taking his cue, fired both barrels. The concussion tore at our ears; as I heard the sound I watched the torso disintegrate into uncountable splinters, blackening the walls when they embedded themselves into the pallor. Lester curled himself against his sister-mannequin's wheels and screamed long and loud. Thatcher let his hand slip from my mouth in his moment of being overcome by the drama; I sank my teeth into the webbing between his thumb and forefinger.

"Goddamn you," I said; before I could move more than a foot away from Thatcher, after he released me, I found Jake at my side, slipping one of his hands into mine, placing the tip of his scalpel at the juncture of my jaw and neck.

"Please, Joanna," he said. "Don't."

"*Jake*," Thatcher said. "Just keep her back."

"Are we quite finished?" Bernard asked, turning away from his microphone. Thatcher wrapped his handkerchief around his injured hand; I hadn't drawn blood.

"Keep her quiet, Jake," Thatcher said. I thought I heard a knock at the room's door; no one else gave signs of having noticed. Bernard tapped the mike with a finger to make certain the equipment hadn't been damaged by the concussion. The music changed; Tallis's forty-part motet spilled its waterfall of voices over us. I watched Avi reload.

"Here comes a chopper to chop off your head," Bernard said, deepening his voice from its natural low baritone into one suitable for a cartoon wolf. "What's the matter, Lester?"

"Please stop—" he said.

"You both hear footsteps again," said Bernard. "Not your father's footsteps. Whose are they? What does your sister do?"

"Makes me hide. In the pantry." Unexpectedly, seeming as a fish cast from water onto land, he began rolling across the floor, coming to rest against the wall opposite from Avi; between them, not three feet from where he lay, was his sister-mannequin. "She stands in the door. In front of me."

"You see her white sweater. The footsteps come closer. You hear them stop. What does your sister say?"

Lester stared up at the mannequin, his eyes as bright with fear as any animal's.

"Thatcher," Bernard said; caught himself. "Lester! What does she say?"

"Stop it," I repeated, attempting to demand, rather than plead; plead I would have done had I thought the response would have been any different. The rap came again at the door. Jake pressed his scalpel against my neck enough that I might know its coldness. "You've done enough to him. Stop it—"

"Answer me," Bernard said, his smile reflecting the shine of the room's constant light.

Thatcher lifted a finger of his unharmed hand to his lips. "Hon," he said, winking at me, "you might learn something if you pay attention."

"Lester!" Bernard shouted, and Lester's reaction was to flatten himself into his wall as if wishing it might swallow him up. Avi took aim. "What does she ask your mother? What does she ask?"

"Why?"

A hail of papier-mâché rained upon Lester, surrounded him within a cloud of plaster-dust. As he screamed he began banging his head against the wall as if trying to smash himself into nonexistence. I slung out my arm, pushing Jake to the floor, and ran to the glass; pounded my fists against its thickness, would surely have broken through had not the doctors and Thatcher and Jake dragged me away, pulling me across the floor, struggling to take me from the room. As he gripped my arms, Thatcher whispered into my ear as if to pass words of love.

"It might be dangerous, interrupting them," he said.

As I heard the music again I remembered the angels I'd been shown.

Spem in alium nunquam habui praeter in te, Deus Israel

I have never put my hope in any other than you, God of Israel

"Your sister's sweater now matches the walls," Bernard said. "Is this any way for a messiah to act, Lester?" Again, Bernard set aside his mike, and spun round in his chair to face us. "Would you please keep it down back there?"

I tried breaking free again; Jake restrained himself, as if in these circumstances he found it impossible to bring the usual end to the confusion. When Thatcher and the doctors got me into the hall we collided with the policeman who'd been knocking at the door.

"Mister Dryden, sir," he said, handing Thatcher a thin sheet of white paper with stripped-away edges. "Emergency, sir. For your attention."

"Your mother sees you, Lester," I heard Bernard say.

"Teletype?" Thatcher muttered to himself, glancing over the paper. "Who'd send anything by—" Allowing the sheet to flutter slowly to the floor he turned on his heels; opened the door that led to the staging area, and went in. Plucking the paper from the air before it landed, I read; realized at once why he'd left. I knew what he intended to do, and couldn't stop him.

"Do you see her?" Bernard said.

FLASH   GET OFF   NXR
     NXR 57E–LA #*($894 FLAH   FLASH FLASH FLASH   FLA

EARTHQUAKE   9.1   RICTER   STRUCK   S   C   ALIF   EPICENT
LAX22993((((((

     GET OFF   GET OFF AND STAY   OFF
     MORE MORE MORE STRUCK 5 30 PST PLS RPT PLS RPT MORE

THOUSANS DEAAAAAAAAAAAAAAAAAAAAAAA

Entering the room I saw Thatcher twisting the shotgun out of Avi's hands. Lester crouched near the mannequins' wheels, tracing his fingertips through the powder and crumbs on the floor. There was a dent in the wall; his hair appeared coated with reddening snow. For the first time he looked so old as he was.

"What are you doing, That—" Bernard began to say. I was reminded of classical scenes of apotheosis when Thatcher fired the gun. Lester flew upward into the air, his arms and legs free of gravity if not inertia; neither seraphim encircled him, nor did cherubim sail round his head; the white sky against which he ascended misted over in a fine red shower. As if in the approach of a tornado pain pressed into my ears; when the sound resounded it came as thunder, deep within the midst of the gale. A thousand bells rang through my head as the noise decayed. Lester descended, thrown from heaven; a babe pitching earthward, end over end. Once he landed I ran to him, hearing nothing but chimes a-buzzing in my brain; I knelt, soaking my clothes in his blood, knowing I could not close the wound in his side. There was nothing to be done that hadn't ensured that it would be done.

"You *idiot*," Bernard screamed. "Thatcher, you fool. What are you doing—"

"You killed her," he bellowed, so consumed by anger he didn't notice Avi yanking the gun away, slinging it across the floor, far from his reach. "Saves her one day, kills her the next. Fucking lying sonofabitch—"

"*Thatcher—!*"

"She's dead, she's dead, I know she's dead—"

"What's he talking about?" Bernard asked. "Thatcher, you idiot—"

Jake entered the room, stopping when he saw blood. Avi steered Thatcher away, holding his arms as he led him out. "You and your fucking God!" he shouted. "I know she's dead. What'll I do—"

"The treatment shouldn't involve the death of the subject," Frank said, his voice calm, what I heard of it; sensed, rather than truly heard. The music played; I found Lester's pulse.

"What'll I do, what—"

"You idiot. You—"

"Japan," Thatcher shouted to anyone listening. "I said Japan—"

Lester's eyes opened as I held him; his lips moved, issuing no words that I could understand. Fearful that my moment's deafness would keep me from hearing what was left to say, I lowered my dead ear until it rested against his lips; heard nothing. Bringing up my arm I readied myself to place my hand over his reopened scar; lifting his own hand, he pushed mine away. Blood came with his words when he finally spoke, and I finally heard.

"Please," he said. "Momma."

"Joanna," Jake said, standing behind us, his voice clear and deep. "Endtime, Joanna. Never need to suffer overlong."

Endtime, yes. Not releasing Lester's hand, scooting out of Jake's way, I nodded, knowing that the spirit, and not the act, mattered, and so gave my blessing to the euthanasia Gus had taught Jake so well. Avi, returning, crossed over to our tableau. My hand was wet with Lester; I thought there could be nothing left in him but his spirit.

"Shema Yisroel," Avi began, in his father's tongue, and as he prayed, I added my parents' voice to his psalm.

"Hear us O Lord," I said, "the Lord thy God is one God."

One in act, in form, if not in spirit: God, Godness, if the act is despicable, how might the spirit save? Jake extended his pinky; its blade shone in the pitiless light. Reaching around Lester's head, he found the spot he sought; then, when Lester left, I felt such heat rise through me. Shortly I thought I should at last combust, and know my flames grow hotter and brighter, until in my incandescence I would burn down the world around me and all who lived in its fire.

"Joanna," Avi said. "Let's go."

Their hands hold the sun, but never burn; Their eyes stare into the fire, but never melt. Their plans proceed as They desire, and not as we would wish them to proceed; neither can Their actions be judged as we would judge our own, nor can They undo what must be done. There was no more reason for Them to answer than there was for us to ask. Take such comfort, then, as can be taken, knowing that those who are gone can never know how much you miss them; Their most difficult lesson is that only by living briefly with others will you at last learn how to live with yourself. They were Two who once were One and would be One again, once the day came. But that day, I knew it was time to go; I had mouths to feed.

TWELVE

· · · · · · · · ·

One day a woman told her daughter a story. "Once I was walking down the avenue and I saw myself coming toward me."

"How is that possible?" her daughter asked.

"Spirits break through from the world of confusion sometimes," she said. "Before she could say anything to me I walked up to her and told her, 'You don't belong here, you. Begone!' She disappeared like fog in the night."

The notion of such comminglings disturbed her daughter. "How do you know you didn't send her out of the world of confusion?"

"Angel," she said, "once you know there is a world of confusion you're no longer in it."

Susie's body deplaned the next morning and, walking on its feet, strolled calmly back to her car; the scientists arrived that afternoon, under separate cover. Her plane prepared to land at the moment the earthquake struck, shaking the field, rocking the control tower; the pilot turned the plane around, that they might reach more solid ground, and so they landed in Salt Lake City. Thatcher was pleased.

No one claimed Lester's body and so he was buried on Hart Island, in the potter's field, on Monday morning. There was no service, not that he would have desired eulogies, nor even wanted me to attend; there would have been no point. As he was laid to rest I was meeting Bernard in a coffee shop on Cedar Street, safely anonymous, alone in the world.

"Look at it this way, sweetness," he said. "Even if he'd been the messiah it would have come to this eventually."

"Tell me what's been going on, Bernard," I said. "After much longer you won't be able."

"Taking more of an interest in your work?" he asked, appearing not entirely pleased. "I'd have never guessed you cared."

"Lying comes to naturally to you now," I explained. "I'd appreciate it if I knew you respected me enough to tell me the truth, one more time. Like you once did."

His coffee's waves broke over the rim of his cup as he lifted it to his mouth. "Ours is a world of artifice, after all," he said. "Mirrors and smoke and mirrors. The question isn't so much what sort of reality can be made, but how much of any reality can anyone deal with, I think. Perhaps we should have asked your boy if you become a saint when nothing surprises you anymore."

"You don't," I said. "Were those papers Avi found forgeries?"

"He did confess to having been approached—"

"Lester always had his reasons for doing things," I said. "When did you have them slipped up there?"

"Thanksgiving morning," he said. "The Irish boy that worked for us last summer, I had him run them up."

"What's real and what's not, Bernard?" I asked. "You even keep Thatcher in the dark about it, don't you?"

"Wouldn't you say it's his element?" he sighed. "You'll be dealing with this soon enough, I suppose. Once I begin programming that damned computer I won't have time to turn around. Bear in mind, though, that particular aspects of this situation can be told to no one beyond this table," he said, looking around; in those days a place such as the one in which we sat was still, usually, safe. "Those who break silence so often wind up broken. You know me too well to know that isn't one of my threats."

"Bernard," I said, "what's truth?"

"I lose track sometimes," he said, looking out the window. "What appears so simple at first can become so complicated. Jensen was involved in a project. He intended to go public about its nature."

"You and Susie are involved in this?"

He set his cup down, spilling coffee into his saucer. "What sort of tricks did Macaffrey teach you—?"

"Call it a hunch. What project are you talking about?"

"You know as I do that were it not for the problem in Long Island there'd be no need for the Army to be in New York anymore. Each year they become more maladjusted and more hardened toward the populace they've been paid by Thatcher to protect—"

"This has to do with something?" I asked.

"With everything," he said, rubbing his eyes with his hands. "It's so typical, isn't it, that for the past thirty years each new President makes the ones who came before look so much better, no matter what they've done? Even that fool Charlie. By managing to get himself nailed up as he did, his example convinced Susan that were our own huddled masses allowed to breathe free they'd swim across the river, march through the streets—carrying heads on pikes for dramatic effect, undoubtedly—and, upon catching our employers, hang them by their feet, Mussolini-style. Soon after we started working there, she told me that an essential aspect of my job was to make certain that the Army would remain in New York for so long as she was alive. Precautions, she said."

"Hasn't the Army grown to appreciate its duties?"

They never imagined they'd have such a time of it. No one in the Defense Department foresaw a local insurrection turning into a prolonged guerrilla war going on just upstream from Washington. A living room war in the truest sense. Army steps up their operations, the insurgents step up theirs. Aerial bombardment has been ongoing over there for the past eleven months. That's ears only—"

"You can hear it at night," I said. "They thought people would think it was firecrackers?"

"Probably. The point is, by rights one-third of the Island's estimated postaccident population should be dead by now. After a specified number of years, with a steady attrition rate dealt upon a fixed population, it would seem that prediction could be made concerning a not-too-distant settlement, or victory. There'd be stragglers, certainly, not unlike those Japanese soldiers in the Pacific that so impress Thatcher. But were nature to take its course the mopping-up could be probably completed within ten years at most. I pointed this out to Susan. Didn't matter. She's crazier than he is, you know."

"What did the two of you come up with?" I asked.

"I came up with it," he said. "A plan by which the Army would never run out of opposition. Jensen oversaw the plan. I oversaw Jensen. She had, and has, no desire to know facts. They're inessential to her beliefs."

"So will you tell me about this plan?" He nodded, and sipped what remained of his coffee.

"A traffic network was already in place. Jensen was familiar with Latin American affairs. All that was required was a readjustment. Fall, chips, where you may. At the time a select group was chosen who might, in the event of inadvertently revealed facts, be held responsible—"

"Otsuka was to take the blame?"

"At the time, we had but a limited understanding of his true influence within his country. Our fault. You kill as many birds as you can with the stones you're given."

"But he wasn't actually involved?"

"Of course not," said Bernard, chewing on one of his nails so intently that I thought I should order breakfast for him. "No problem, early on. Suddenly he becomes the key to settling our difficulties, or should I say Thatcher's difficulties, with Japan. Everything started coming loose at the seams—"

"What was readjusted, Bernard?"

"Cargo," he said. "The network continued transporting cargo from south to north along standard routes. We shipped a different product."

"What?"

"Thatcher's xenophobia is an awful thing," he said, resting his chin in his hand as he propped his elbow on the tabletop. "These immigration quotas he's insisted upon for the indefinite future. Can you imagine the potential going to waste, forced to remain in the wilds? For better or worse, Joanna, America is still better than most. Even now half the world would move here if they could. Granted, that says more about the world than about America. Still, I knew there had to be a way to do what she wanted and give at least a few to have their chance as well . . ."

"You're moving people?"

He nodded. "In small boats. They have supercharged engines and Stealth siding to elude Navy patrols. The Coast Guard never touches anything of ours and never has, those we don't worry about."

"Shipping them from Guyana to Connecticut."

"That's one route," he said. "Each boat carries from seventy to one hundred and fifty-five, depending upon the layout of the decks. It's a three-day trip, generally—"

"Three days and a twenty-five percent loss during the trip," I said. His fingertip bled, as if he were stricken with an errant stigmata. "Jensen went to Mystic not long ago, I gather, or one of the other ports. A shipment came in while he was there. He went to inspect the cargo. Is that what happened?" Bernard appeared more than unnerved that I'd become as accomplished at inference as Lester. With idle, unwounded fingers he straightened his necktie. "Then he threatened to go public?"

"It was his own fault," said Bernard. "You have to delegate responsibility, you have to. Like you, he didn't always follow the soundest advice he heard."

"Who was he going to tell?" I asked. "Who couldn't you have bought off? Who would have cared enough?" He didn't answer. "Thatcher? He doesn't know—?"

"She told me he'd disapprove," Bernard said. "She says it's as important that he never find out as it is that the Army not leave. That's easy enough to accomplish as long as everyone behaves as they should behave. When Jensen developed this newfound aversion to his project he let me know how he felt. Perhaps I didn't treat his opinion with as much respect as he believed it deserved. Before he left for Chicago he let his feelings slip in such a way that it became evident to me he was preparing to tell Thatcher, upon his return. At my request Gus killed him for being a spy for Otsuka. At least, that's what I told Gus." He tapped his fingers against the side of his head. "That excuse served as well for Avi, when Gus's turn came."

"Why did you drag Lester into this?" I asked. "Why was it necessary?"

"He insisted upon leading Thatcher down roads there was no need for him to be traveling. And you're well aware of my doubts concerning that entire operation. Doomed from the start. It seemed a convenient way to kill two birds with one stone, and I don't mean that literally—"

"Killed or driven mad," I said.

"Certainly not the former," he said. "Not necessarily the latter, but—"

"You enjoyed doing that to him, Bernard. Why? How did he hurt you?"

"I didn't like what he was doing to you," Bernard said. "I never meant that he should be killed. I'm not Thatcher, for God's sake."

The weather that morning was winterlike, in the traditional sense, as it once had always been in November. It no longer felt appropriate to the season. I said nothing, neither denying nor agreeing; there was little that Bernard so despised as much as silence.

"I'm not Thatcher, Joanna," he repeated, as if it were one of Avi's less obscure mantras, a chant with which he might heal, a litany to sway the hearts of the heathen; a song sung silently in the brain, reminding him of where he'd been, and who he was with, when first he heard it.

"Let me see if I understand, then," I said. "I suppose much of the cargo comes from South America, but I can't see Dryco limiting itself. Where else, Bernard? The Caribbean, I'm sure. Africa? Asia?"

"People will do anything to come to America."

"When they already live in the Bronx?" I asked, recalling that white van's red cross. "When they reach America what happens?"

"They're transferred into smaller boats—"

"Those who survived."

"Those," he said. "They're offloaded in stages at night, along the North Fork. Then the boats go back—"

"Leaving them on the beach to enjoy their new life in America?"

"Joanna—"

"What's the survival rate for the first week, Bernard?"

"Keep your voice down—"

"It's not only men, I'm sure. Or adults. I'd think it'd be most cost-effective to transfer whole families. Any package deals offered?" He looked away from me. "Weekend rates? Can't you see what you're doing?"

"What chance do they have where they were?" he asked. "What opportunity? They have a chance here, Joanna. They really do. The best always come out of it all right. What chance would they otherwise have?"

"Have you ever seen them being brought in?" I asked. "Have you?"

"It's an untenable position I'm in, Joanna," he said. "You bring profit out of loss when you can. Draw good from bad. You know."

His words sounded so rational, so heavenly, that had I not seen the face from which they issued, nor known the act, I might have been confused as to whose spirit spoke, to what purpose, to the living. "You've managed to keep the Army from discovering this arrangement? I shouldn't think they'd think much of it."

"Several commanders in useful positions have enough of a notion to take their payment and keep quiet," he said; taking another drink from his cup, his face sagged, discovering his coffee had cooled. "They believe it's useful, having a training field so close. Prepares the boys for anything, one told me—"

"Have the shipments stopped—?"

"Certainly not," he said.

"With Susie's knowledge?"

"With her blessing," he said. It was nearly nine, I saw, reading the clock on the wall; almost time to go. There were several people I still needed to see. "Normality proceeds," he continued. "The caravans bark, the dogs move on. I'm sorry, Joanna."

"I am, too—"

"It strikes me that you've grown into your position," he said. The restaurant began emptying out; the food was nearly gone, and they would receive no more until noontime. Bernard glanced at the window, at the multitudes passing. "Oh, Joanna," he said. "The world would be such a lovely place without these people in it."

Returning to the office, I found all progressing as it always did: secretaries typed memos, mailroom staff brought deliveries, comptrollers oversaw the growth of ever-increasing numbers, bookkeepers peered at their terminals, assistants stood round the coffeemakers, pouring fresh cups. From seven continents came calls and faxes and messages, and the Dryden Corporation continued upon its appointed task, to remake the world in its image, to join what was once apart, to separate what was meant to be together. Avi sat on one of the sofas in Thatcher's waiting room perusing magazines, awaiting his cue. He didn't see me when I came in; he stood when he heard me speak, his manners, as ever, unfailing.

"Thatcher's in?" I asked Lilly, his secretary. With a jerk of her head she nodded toward his door, and continued typing at her keyboard, her eyes set upon her screen. She wore plastic splints attached to her arms, so that her wrists could have more support, if no less pain, while she typed.

"He and Mrs. D," she said. Before I went in I paused to see what Avi had to say for himself, and to say what I needed to him.

"You're all right?" he asked. "I was concerned."

"I'm sure. How's Thatcher and the little woman?"

"Celebratory in a quiet way," he said. "They're going over some new projects, I believe. You'll be told shortly, no doubt—"

"I'm giving notice today," I said. "I'm leaving, Avi."

His expression remained as stolid as it ever was; his eyes alone revealed the surprise he felt. He cocked his head to one side, as if adjusting for deafness, and knowing where best he could ascertain what he heard. "When?"

"As soon as I quit," I said. "I'll be here another hour, maybe."

"What'll you do?"

"I have to leave, Avi. This sort of thing isn't what I'm meant for. I'll be fine—"

"What they did to Macaffrey," he said, forgetting his presence at the event. "It wasn't right."

"You were doing your job," I said. "I don't hold it against you."

He shifted his weight from foot to foot as he stood there, now seeming almost anxious to break away, to begin another conversation with another person, or perhaps only to return to his work. "It does seem he was something other than what we were led to believe."

"He was," I said.

"You'll have to give up your apartment," he said. "Where'll you stay? Joanna, you can't live on the street—"

"I'm going away for a while," I said. "It's hard to say when I'll be back in town. It won't be very long, but—"

"Will I see you again?"

"I don't know," I said. "Perhaps you shouldn't expect to." There were moments, during the time I knew Avi, when his transcendent enclosure—his aura, one might put it—would without warning disappear, leaving him as helpless as an oyster removed from its shell. He knew such a moment, just then, and said nothing; I knew how he felt. "It's my life, Avi. You say I have to accept it for what it is, and it's not here. Not anymore."

"People adapt," he said. "It takes time—"

"They try to adapt," I said. "Some do better than others. Give my best to your father. I'm sorry I never met him."

"It's as well," Avi said. "He wouldn't have liked you."

"There's something I'm sure you know that I need to tell you," I said. He stared into my eyes, for once, possibly, not seeing in them a reflection of himself. "When the moment comes, Jake'll kill you. He knows what you did."

"I am aware of that," he said. "I don't want to know when it'll be before it happens—"

"I wouldn't tell you if I could," I said. "Just one day you'll not even know he's there."

"There's a better way?" he asked, and shrugged. I kissed him and walked toward Thatcher's door. "Take care," he said. "Find peace."

"I have."

As I entered Thatcher's office I saw the Drydens behind his desk, she perched next to him; their feet touched, propped upon its surface. There was nothing so heartening as seeing two people together who so personified the Platonic ideal, that those whose souls were split apart in the life before birth might, through predestination or serendipity or happenstance, find one another in this world and so rejoin their spirit even if, in time, their conjuncture destroyed them. Several seconds went by before my presence intruded upon their silent rapture; had I desired, and had I better learned my corporate lessons, I could have killed them both before they even said hello.

"Look who's here," said Thatcher. "Hon, how you doing? You okay?" I nodded. "You sure? Ready to get back to work yet or you think you need a little more time off? What's today? Monday? Come in tomorrow, why not?"

"I won't be in tomorrow, Thatcher," I said.

"Well," he said, "we do need to get the train back on the track around here, but if you need longer—"

"I'm resigning."

"I didn't catch that, hon."

"You did, Thatcher. I'm leaving your employ. Effective immediately."

"Wait a minute. Come on in here and sit down. Talk to me about this." He turned to his wife, who looked no worse for her stumbles at the edge; without a word she stood, smoothed her skirt and picked up her newspaper.

"You'll be missed," she said to me, her look focused upon the distance, seeming more than one who had merely chosen blindness; resembling, almost, one of Lester's children, one born without eyes but taught never to seek the light. Once she closed the door behind her Thatcher patted the warmed seat next to him.

"Communication's the key in business, hon. Talk to me."

"I'll stand—"

"Then stand closer. You thought about this? Don't you think this might be a little rash?"

"I've been thinking about it for some time, Thatcher, and I've made up my mind. There's nothing left to talk about. I only wanted to give notice—"

"Mighty short notice," he said. "You haven't got anything set up elsewhere that I've heard about." His statement came as declaration rather than question. "What's made you do this? What set it off?"

"You have to ask?" He seemed utterly, truly baffled; his feigned behavior came more naturally to him than the actual—had almost supplanted it entirely, I believed.

"Joanna," he said. "I told you I was sorry, and I meant it."

"You mean it as you say it, Thatcher. Then it's gone."

"Something snaps in my head when I think something's the matter with Pussums," he said, using the name I knew he used for his wife when he dealt most intimately with her; twice, with me, he'd cried out that name at the crescendo of his joy, surely forgetting in that moment that I was even in the room. "Who else did I have to go after? Who'd I have to blame, hon? You can't blame God."

"You mean you can't kill God." He had no reply to that; perhaps he had someone working on the problem even as we spoke.

"I don't know what else to tell you," he said. "Even if he

didn't seem to be making himself especially useful, it was still counterproductive to have disposed of him."

"That it was."

"My temper'll get me in deep one day," he said. "I just thought she was gone. What would I do without her?"

"One day she will be gone," I said. "What then?"

"You don't think I'm upset about this?" It was reassuring to see such consistency in one man's soul. "You know how I am. I try to let my emotions out when they ought to come out, but sometimes they just spill all over the place."

"Well, I can't do the job anymore, Thatcher. It's time for me to go. Nothing either of us can say will change that."

"You oughta keep your options open," he said. "It's a bad world out there if you don't have a helping hand, hon. Getting worse all the time."

"You'd see to it if it wasn't, of course."

He held out his hands, as if to take mine from me; opened them, palms up, in a display of supplicance. "Omelets need eggs, hon, omelets need eggs. How're you going to get by? You need anything—?"

"No," I said, dropping my apartment keys and my corporate signifyers onto his desk, keeping for the moment only the card that allowed me access into my office. "I have to clean out my desk and then I'll be going."

"You've left me speechless," he said, leaning back in his chair. "It's all too sudden."

"Things happen, Thatcher."

"Joanna," he said, "something I've always wanted to tell you—"

"What?" I asked, not yet leaving; certainly it shouldn't have been hope that caused me to linger, one second more.

"I never really did think you ever put your heart into this, hon," he said. "You can't go halfway and get anywhere."

I almost laughed; didn't; couldn't. "I know. I'll stop off in Security so they can remove me from the records. I know it's required."

"I'd have trusted you to do that, hon," he said. "It'll be hard living without you."

"You'll manage." He smiled, and nodded to himself. It pleased him when people accepted his worth. I closed his door, and walked to my office.

Desks breed trash as closets breed hangers; from the drawers of mine I drew forth and disposed a hundred restaurants' matchbooks, long-forgotten memos from Finance concerning medical bills, programs from events unimportant at the time, and less so now; old disks, empty boxes once housing pens, three dozen copies of my resumé in various states. A memo Bernard sent to me on our first day at Dryco marked a page in the Executive Health Plan Guide; he wrote it down, having not yet ascertained if the offices were bugged.

At least we're working.

The page marked concerned obstetrical care. Into the bin all went; what I had at home could now be dispersed as easily as Jensen's had been, as his grandmother's had been, as Gus's would be. Hard copy memories so transmogrify with time: notes fade until the words written are not so unreadable as incomprehensible; letters of love undergo a reverse metamorphosis, dropping their brilliant wings within safely sealed cocoons and emerging, if broken into, as something to crawl over the skin at night; only photographs, as those in more primitive cultures believed, catch a shard of the soul of the one photographed, nonetheless memorable only to those who were there at the time.

"Joanna."

Jake startled me, knocking on the doorframe at my office's entrance; he clung to its side, as if fearful to enter without an invitation.

"Come in, Jake. It's all right."

"Why the open road?" he asked, stepping in cautiously, as if uncertain who else might be in there with me.

"It lies before me," I said, placing my purse beneath my desk. In it were snapshots, combs, two dozen credit cards, my licenses, my makeup, one hundred new dollars; my earthly possessions, all unnecessary. "Come to say good-bye?"

"To escort out," he said. He'd had a new cast applied, I noticed, a simpler splint free of obvious hazard. "Forgive what was necessary."

"Don't look so sad, Jake," I said. "Your face will freeze like that. You did what you should have." As he stood there I thought he might be wondering why he should disagree. I shredded my superfluous documents.

"I'll miss you overmuch," he said.

"I'm sure you miss Gus more than you'll miss me."

"No," he said. "Why waste the look when you won't see the bullet?"

"That's so."

"You vizzed ahead?" he asked. "That they'd take Macaffrey?"

"It was too late to stop it, even before it happened. Do you understand that?" He nodded.

"What now?"

"Getting out of town. A clear life ensuing," I said. "What strength I have's my own."

Jake smiled, recognizing my quotes. "Flying?" he asked.

"You know a better way?"

His grin was that of a boy much younger than he could ever be again. The windows in the Dryco building were hermetically sealed so that on days when the air conditioning faltered the place might quickly become more unbearable than it already was. As Jake sat down on the couch I walked across my office, to my own window, one not nearly so large as any of Thatcher's. The drapes had to come down to be laundered anyway.

"Joanna," he said, "What's desired? I'll do—"

I climbed up, stepping into the niche between wall's edge and windowpane. Reaching high above my head I disconnected the hooks; the veil dropped away. From my new vantagepoint I saw city, land, and ocean; saw the curve of the world and the unceilinged sky.

"Joanna," Jake said. "Head floorways. You'll fall—"

Lester came to earth, lived and died. Who doesn't? I didn't.

"Joanna—!"

So through winter morning I flew on alone. A snowfall of glass showered down, chiming as it drifted toward the street far below. Sparrows and gulls and doves circled round me, their wings so like those of angels. The mist of the clouds wet my face as I cried: cried for my friends, for my parents, for the millions of this city of God; for those who were lost, for those who would never be found. The tears I shed for Lester were ones of joy. There could be no separation from him; that which once was one would soon be one again. On the desolate isle a river's width away I'd wait until the day came, and then return that our world might be recovered: our sick world, our wonderful world, our blessed world that wept for its mother. Our first night together, Lester told me what I once knew I'd hear; I'd always wanted to hear, and see, and remember all I'd known. You're the Messiah, he told me, and I remembered, and I knew. You're the Messiah, he told me; I'd always been the Messiah.

AUTHOR'S NOTE

Those of you who have now read my three novels surely perceive that these books are not so disconnected as certain of their characters.

If *Heathern* is the first or, for that matter, second exposure you have had to my particular virus, I should recommend that you now read, or reread, in this order, *Ambient* and *Terraplane*.

Elvissey, the next book of the three remaining to be written within this six-part ensemble, takes place fifteen years after *Terraplane*, and will as ever tell of people who should have known better, and the worlds they make for themselves.

THE BEST IN SCIENCE FICTION